ENTANGLED HEARTS

YAHRAH ST.JOHN

OLIVER
HEBER
BOOKS

Published by Oliver-Heber Books

0 9 8 7 6 5 4 3 2 1

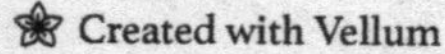

Created with Vellum

1

"Great show, Chynna!"

"Way to go, Chynna!"

"Love your music."

Chynna gave one of her megawatt smiles to the screams of adoring fans, who were calling out her name and giving her "attaboys" backstage at the Staples Center in early February. The adoration used to be the part of show business she loved the most, but over the years, her love for it all had started to fade. Too much time on the road, too many concerts, too many failed relationships, and she'd become jaded.

"Thank you, thank you." Chynna stopped to sign autographs as she made her way down the long corridor to her dressing room, even though her bodyguards tried to spur her along.

"Just a second." She gave a fan a huge hug, and the young girl took a photo with her cell phone.

Who would have ever thought I would've gotten this far? She and her mother had traveled across Tennessee hitting every bar and nightclub hoping for "the big break" until, finally, she was discovered singing the national anthem in a mall in Memphis. She'd signed a record contract before she had time to think about signing with another agency. Her first single had hit the Billboard Hot 100 instantly and propelled her into superstardom. Her next four singles had hit the top of the charts, and her debut album had gone Platinum.

Then her second album had come. It was a departure from her artistic and highly acclaimed first album because Elias Ross, "Eli" for short, had pushed her into making songs that were more commercial. Eli was one of the owners of the record label and had appointed himself the head of artist development. His vision couldn't be further from what Chynna wanted, but she was still new to the business and tried to make every effort to get along. She didn't want to be considered a diva.

Chynna hadn't been happy about it. *Why change a good thing?* "The public wants more sex appeal, more heat," they'd said. If she wanted to compete with the Beyoncés and Rihannas of the world, she had to up her game. And so she'd begun dressing in bustiers, stilettos and cut-out swimsuits and splashing around with hot guys in pools to sex up her image. She'd had to hit the gym hard with a personal trainer to keep herself fit and feel comfortable showing off that much skin.

Her next album had built on the success of the first two and had gone Multi-Platinum. Chynna James had her pulse on what was current, the industry had said. Now she was on a twenty-city tour promoting her third album, hoping to make it as successful as her previous work. The first two singles had already hit number one on the charts. And tonight, she'd debuted her third single. The crowd had seemed to enjoy the up-tempo song and had jumped to its feet and danced in the aisles of the stadium with Chynna and her male backup dancers.

Now the fans were complimenting her. "Loved the new single," another fan yelled as she finally made it to Chynna's dressing room.

"Thank you." Chynna smiled and slid inside the quiet of the room.

She glanced at all five foot six of herself in the mirror. Her big honey-blond hair was still holding up after a two-hour concert. Beads of perspiration dotted her overly made-up face. The outfit she wore was one of many spiked-out and bedazzled getups she paraded in onstage.

Penelope Banks, her personal assistant, handed her a towel and a bottle of Evian, which Chynna immediately started chugging. Then she wiped the sweat off her brow with the towel and tossed it aside.

"That was a great show," her manager, Deacon Clark, said as he knocked on her dressing room door and entered without waiting for a response.

"Did you hear the applause? Apparently, they loved the new single," Chynna responded, glancing up at him.

Deacon wasn't much in the looks department. He was bald, five foot seven with a slender build, and wore glasses; but he had a good heart. Deacon had been her manager from the beginning. When Eli had sent managers over for Chynna to interview, it was her mother who'd said Deacon was the one. And Chynna found him to be a straight shooter ever since.

"See?" Deacon said. "And you were worried it was too much of a dance single."

"True, but I don't want the fans to forget that I can sing too."

"And they won't," Deacon promised.

Chynna didn't think that was true, but she dropped the subject. "What's on tap for tomorrow?"

"You have dance rehearsal for the music video for your second single, and you have reading of the script for the movie," Penelope answered.

Penelope was one of many, from Deacon to her publicist, Fiona, who kept Chynna on task. How else would she remember the endless duties of being a Multi-Platinum phenomenon? Although taller than Chynna, Penelope was a full-figured black woman but was afraid to show it. She dressed simply in a silk blouse and trousers. Her only true sign of personality was that she kept her hair natural in funky twists, contrasting Chynna's endless weaves and wigs.

"Do I really?" Chynna sighed dramatically as she laid her head back on the sofa. For her first movie, she'd been given the coveted role of a down-on-her-luck superstar in need of a comeback. She'd been pushed into doing the film by the record label in order to expand her horizons and raise her profile. She wasn't very good at it because she didn't really like acting. Chynna suspected Eli had pulled strings to get her the gig over better, more established actresses. The gossip certainly was that there had been some shenanigans and Chynna wasn't up to snuff.

The film required her to be vulnerable yet gritty, and Chynna wasn't altogether sure she could do it; but if nothing else in this business, she'd learned to fake it until she made it. *So what if I'm not the best actress in the world?* She was taking acting lessons as instructed by Lucas Kingston, the man behind R&K Records. "R" stood for Eli Ross and "K" stood for Kingston.

"Yeah, you do," Deacon stated firmly, backing up Penelope on Chynna's obligation to show up for the dance rehearsal and script reading.

"If you insist." Chynna rolled her eyes upward.

"I do. Acting is the next logical step in your career

and your brand. Your signature perfume is almost ready, and we're already in talks with a designer for your clothing line."

"Now that idea," Chynna said, pointing her finger at Deacon, "I love." She'd always had an affinity for fashion, and her style was copied by millions of her fans.

"Good, because we'll need you to meet with them in a couple of weeks to review their designs," Deacon replied.

"Good. Now leave me be so I can shower and get changed."

Deacon departed, but Penelope remained behind long enough to say, "I've laid out your favorite velour jumpsuit."

"Thanks, Penelope. You're a doll." Chynna waved her hand so Penelope could depart.

After she left, Chynna let out a heavenly sigh. She was finally alone. She'd struggled getting through the concert, and her entire entourage was oblivious to the fact that she was burned out. She'd been on the road for the better part of the last two years, trying to get over Lamar Hobbs, the man who'd broken her heart. She was exhausted mentally and physically.

Lamar had been one of her backup singers, and Chynna hadn't noticed him at first because she'd been so focused on her first album and making it a success. But eventually, Lamar had wormed his way into her heart *and* her bed. With being discovered so young, she'd had very little time to date, so Lamar was her first real relationship. He had a sexy grin and a body for seduction. It had been all hard lines and angles, and the sex was so damn good. Lamar had been Chynna's first, which meant she'd fallen head over heels for his smoothing-talking ass.

She'd been devastated to learn he'd been playing her long enough to get ahead. Once he'd obtained his own record contract, he'd given her the kiss-off. His timing couldn't have been worse because she and her twin, Kenya, had learned their mother was dying of terminal cancer. Losing Lamar and her mother had been a double whammy, and Chynna had never taken the time to properly grieve. Eli had insisted the best way to avoid depression was to work on another album, so she'd thrown herself into her work. And now ... now Chynna wanted out, but how? She didn't see a way out, but when the time came, she would take it. The consequences be damned.

"AGAIN." The director, Carter Wright, motioned with his hands for Chynna to reread her lines on Monday afternoon. "For Christ's sake, I need more heart, Chynna. More passion."

"I'm trying," Chynna said, frustrated. She'd read through her scene twice already, and he still wasn't satisfied. She jumped out of her seat in the conference room where she and the entire cast were doing a read-through of the movie. She flipped over her chair in the process, then fled the room for some air. She heard the whispers of "diva" as she left.

Her co-star and love interest in the movie, Blake Cooper, followed her. Blake was classically handsome, with caramel-colored skin as smooth as a baby's bottom. He was over six feet tall with deep-set brown eyes, curly lashes and a killer smile. All the ladies adored Blake. He'd been named the sexiest man alive by *People* magazine the previous year and women were lined up to get next to him. Chynna wasn't one of them and that seemed to make Blake all the more interested in her. He was too clean-cut for her. She needed someone manly, a little more ... rugged.

Chynna glanced sideways at Blake as he followed her down the corridor. "You really needn't have followed me."

"You looked upset," Blake said, peering down at her.

Chynna kept walking until they were outside of earshot of any of the other actors. She stopped in front of the bench outside the production building and took a seat.

"I'm not upset," Chynna stated emphatically. "I just don't understand what he's looking for."

"Acting can be hard." Blake touched her thigh as he sat down next to her. "You have to know when to be subtle and when to put it all on the line."

"I thought that's what I was doing."

"Hmm ... not so much," Blake admitted. "But I would be willing to run lines with you in private if you'd like."

"Is that so?" Chynna said, glancing up at him through mascara-coated eyelashes.

"I was nominated for a Golden Globe and SAG award last year," Blake replied.

Chynna smiled. Actors were just like singers—you had to stroke their enormous egos. "Oh, that's right. Running lines might help, because Carter doesn't think I know anything. Maybe he's right." It was the first time in her life she'd ever doubted herself. Music she knew. She knew what was expected of her, but acting was something different altogether. She wanted to be the best, but she was tanking the reading.

"Carter can be a hardass," Blake admitted, "but that's only because he wants you to give your best performance."

"What if I can't give it?" Chynna asked, looking over at Blake.

Blake reached out and tucked a wayward strand of Chynna's honey-blond hair behind her ear. "You can do this," he said. "You just have to believe you can, and everyone else will believe it too."

Chynna looked up at Blake and felt complete faith and trust in him. He seemed so kind, so understanding and so compassionate, which is why it came as a complete shock when he lowered his head to brush his lips softly across hers in a gentle, yet persuasive kiss. Blake was attractive, but he was also very married and his actions repulsed her.

Chynna pulled away and jumped off the bench. "What the hell do you think you're doing?"

Blake seemed startled by her outburst. "Kissing you, which I thought was going rather well until you interrupted us."

Chynna ran her hands through her honey-blond hair and searched around to see if anyone had seen them. "Blake, you're married."

Blake shrugged. "In name only. Giselle and I don't have a real marriage. We're like two ships passing in the night. One of us is always eager to one-up the other in our career."

"Well I don't want to be in the middle of your drama," Chynna replied, "so leave me out of it." She stormed away, oblivious to the photographer hidden in the bushes who'd just photographed their entire encounter.

"CHYNNA, CHYNNA, CHYNNA!!" Hearing the screams of someone calling out her name was usually a welcome sound to Chynna James, but not now. Several muscled bodyguards chaperoned her as she rushed from her chauffeured Jeep into her ten-bedroom mansion to escape the reporters who'd been cataloguing her every move since the story of her supposed affair with Blake had broken several days ago. They were like vultures, ready to pick her bones bare if she gave one inch.

Blake had misconstrued her self-doubt in her acting ability as a reason to plant a smooch on her that the press just so happened to catch on camera. Now she was being touted on every entertainment television show and newspaper rag as a slut and homewrecker, which she absolutely was not. She would never dream of doing the same thing to another woman that her father had done to her mother, Ava James.

Her father had cheated and added insult to injury by leaving his wife and two young daughters with nothing so that he could live with the other woman. But that hadn't stopped Chynna's mother from working hard to ensure that she and her sister, Kenya, had the best in life. When Chynna wanted singing lessons, her mother worked an extra shift. When Kenya wanted acting lessons, her mother worked double shifts. Nothing had been out of reach for her two girls. That's why being a successful R&B singer and now an actress was so important to Chynna—because she'd come from nothing.

Kenya hadn't fared as well as Chynna with her ambitions. She was a struggling actress on an acclaimed cable dramedy series, but she hadn't made "that big break" into the movies yet. Chynna felt guilty that she'd been given the coveted role in her new film when Kenya was the better actress.

But this bad press was not good for her image *or* the movie. *Damn that Blake!* She was no more interested in him than in any of the other would-be suitors Eli had put in front of her. The man she really wanted was Lucas Kingston.

Now him, she wouldn't mind being accused of having an affair with. That man turned her on all kinds of crazy. He exuded a certain male aura of swagger and confidence that Chynna found hard to resist. But resist he had. Despite her best efforts to seduce Lucas, he'd shown absolutely zero interest in her, and that perplexed and surprised Chynna. She was used to men and even women of all races and ages fawning all over her, but Lucas was the one person who could care less about her fame and fortune, which was why she was so upset by this Blake incident.

Lucas would not be pleased to see his most famous —or was that *infamous*? —star on the covers of the news magazines in a compromising position. She wanted to convince Lucas she was more than just a pretty face with big boobs and long legs who pranced around on stage and in music videos. She wanted him to see she was a smart, capable business woman and aspiring actress.

No such luck. Chynna threw down one of the weekly tabloids in a huff and strolled out onto the balcony of her estate. She wanted to strangle the bastard for ruining her otherwise pristine reputation. Sure, she was known for her sexy clothes and her endless parade of boyfriends, but *homewrecker*? Chynna thought about going over to Blake's condo and giving him a piece of her mind, but that would only add fuel to the fire. The press was already camped out on her doorstep. If her car as so much went in that direction, the TMZs and other reporters would be on her Jeep so fast she'd probably get in a wreck trying to escape them and that she didn't need ... then it dawned on her.

She needed her twin. Kenya would be able to calm her frayed nerves and offer her some words of wisdom. Kenya had always been the levelheaded one, and Chynna prayed today would be no different. She rushed back inside, grabbed her iPhone and threw herself down on the king-sized, four-poster canopy bed in her master bedroom.

Chynna dialed Kenya's cell, praying her sister would pick up.

"Hello."

"It's me."

"Chynna, how are you, twinie?" Kenya said. At the euphemism that only Kenya used, Chynna smiled, and instantly, her heart softened.

"Hey, twinie."

"I suppose you're calling because of the press?" Kenya surmised.

"Am I that obvious?"

"Uh, yeah." Kenya laughed heartily into the phone. "I know you better than anyone else and your face, *our* face, is all over TV and the Internet. People in the grocery store were giving me the stank eye. An old lady came up to me today while I was standing in line paying for my purchases and hit me with her handbag and told me 'Shame on you.'"

Chynna sighed. "I am so sorry, sis, to put you in the middle of this."

"Yeah, well, people sometimes forget that you have an identical twin," Kenya replied. "I guess when you're on a small-time TV show that no one watches, you're invisible." She laughed bitterly.

"But it's such a good show," Chynna said.

"That no one is watching," Kenya repeated. "But

enough about me. How the hell did you get yourself into this mess?"

"It's stupid, really," Chynna said. "I was talking with Blake and lamenting how bad I was at acting, and he tried to comfort me."

"You don't say?"

"Don't be sarcastic. It doesn't suit you," Chynna returned. "Anyway, here I was all down-and-out, and he plants a kiss on me that the paparazzi just happened to catch on film."

"Oh Lord, so what are you going to do?"

"Lay low," Chynna replied, "until the heat dies down."

"As if that's possible, Chynna. You're the most well-known singer in the country right now. Your last five singles have hit number one on the Billboard charts. Everyone knows you."

"Doesn't matter," Chynna said, sitting up quickly on her bed. "I have to get out of Dodge and quick. I was thinking about going to that spa you wanted to go to last year for our birthday that I had to bail on."

"I don't know," Kenya said skittishly.

Chynna could completely understand. She'd felt terrible about canceling their birthday plans for a last-minute gig on the Oscars. Their first-choice singer turned up ill, and Eli and even Lucas had insisted she perform. "This is a great opportunity to cement yourself as here to stay. You have to strike while the iron is hot and take your fifteen minutes of fame," Lucas had said.

Chynna wanted more than fifteen minutes. She wanted a long career like Whitney or Mariah. So she'd canceled the day before she and Kenya were due to meet at Canyon Ranch spa in Arizona. Kenya had been furious with her and hadn't spoken to her for weeks, even after Chynna had sent her the new Louis Vuitton purse and matching luggage. Kenya had returned it unopened and told her she couldn't buy her forgiveness.

"I promise this won't be like before," Chynna pleaded.

"Don't make promises you can't keep," Kenya replied tartly.

Her words stung, but Chynna took them in stride. "And you're right, but I'm telling you, twinie, I can't take this. My house is besieged. They're probably going through my garbage as we speak, trying to find some evidence of a supposed affair, and if they can't find that, they'll fabricate it. I need you, Kenya."

Kenya must have heard the desperation in Chynna's voice because she relented. "Alright, alright," she said. "I'll come with you. When do we leave?"

"I DON'T THINK this is a wise decision," Deacon said later that day when Chynna informed him of her decision as she packed her Louis Vuitton suitcases. "I think you need to stay in town and fight. You need to meet with Oprah or sit down with one of the morning shows and tell your side of things before this story spirals out of control."

"I agree with Deacon on this," Chynna's publicist, Fiona, said. "We're in major damage control."

Fiona was a slender redhead with brilliant blue eyes. She wore nothing but designer suits and had a fetish for Louboutin shoes and Brighton jewelry. She might seem unassuming at first glance, but when pushed, Fiona was a barracuda.

"Chynna, you know I'm not just your manager, but your friend, and this is serious," Deacon started.

"You're in the middle of your first movie role that hasn't even started filming yet. If you get caught in the middle of a scandal, they could rescind the offer."

Chynna's eyes grew large with fear. "You really think they would do that?"

"Image is everything in this town," Fiona said, backing up Deacon. "Some celebs have survived the scandal, but many others never recover."

"And you have a morals clause in your contract," Deacon added. "And we had to fight awfully hard to get you the role over other actresses."

Chynna read between the lines of what Deacon *wasn't* saying. "You mean better actresses," she stated.

Deacon shrugged.

Chynna couldn't be angry with him. From the beginning of their professional relationship, she'd always asked Deacon to be honest with her—brutally honest. And Deacon always did exactly that. He was right about her acting, but that didn't mean she didn't have to like it. "You may be right," she finally said, "but I've made my decision."

"What about the record label?" Deacon asked. "What do you suggest I tell them?"

"Nothing."

"Excuse me?" Deacon peered at her.

"You heard right," Chynna replied. "You work *for me* not them. I don't want them to know where I'm at. When this blows over in a couple of weeks, I'll come back and do as you suggest."

"Lucas will not be happy about this."

Chynna thought about the gorgeous music mogul and hated doing anything that would hinder her ultimate goal of being in his bed and on his arm. "I don't care, but you reveal my whereabouts to no one, including Lucas."

. . .

TWO HUNDRED MILES from Los Angeles in Tucson, Arizona, Noah Hart stared into the eyes of a stubborn Egyptian Arabian horse at his family's ranch. He'd been trying to tame the thoroughbred for weeks with no success. He'd never met a more stubborn female than perhaps his late wife, Maya, the love of his life.

They'd met in the sixth grade when he'd walked her home from school after several boys teased her about being too much of a tomboy. Maya had loved doing anything a boy her age would and hadn't been afraid to show it. He'd always loved her fire and her spirit. She'd been ready to take on the three boys who'd teased her about not being able to spit or throw a fastball as fast as they did, but lucky for her, Noah had stepped in.

Maya hadn't been happy about the interference, just as this damn horse was not happy about being led by the bridle in Noah's hands. "I don't need you to fight my battles" she'd said. "I can take care of myself."

"Sure you could," he'd countered. "But it's always nice to have backup." She'd captured his heart and he'd been besotted with her until the day she died in a car accident that also claimed their unborn child.

Now, he stood ready for battle, ready to do anything to get this stubborn horse to conform.

"Noah, leave that horse be," his sister, Rylee, said with a slight Southern drawl from the other side of the fence she was perched on. "She'll come to you when she's good and ready."

"Stay out of this, Rylee. I can handle her," he yelled over his back.

"Who's the vet in this scenario?" she responded tartly, reminding him that she had a degree in veterinarian medicine from Texas A & M University. But so what he didn't have some fancy degree? He'd been working on the ranch since he was waist-high, following their father, Isaac, around, and learning the cattle and oil business. So there was nothing he didn't know about animals that Rylee could tell him, no matter how well- intentioned.

"That may very well be the case, doc, but I've got this. Why don't you go on and take care of that cow that's about to give birth to twin calves?"

"Humph." He heard Rylee's comment as he dismissed her concerns, but she rightly knew when to press an issue and when to leave him alone.

It had been two years since Maya died, but Noah's nerves were still raw and testy. He couldn't believe God could be so cruel to take away the two things he loved more than anything or anyone in this world, save for his family and the ranch. It seemed like a cruel twist of fate to learn he'd lost Maya to brain death and that the baby's chances of making it to term were slim to none.

She'd been five months pregnant, and a fetus needed to be at least six months for any chance of survival outside the womb. The doctors had indicated they couldn't deliver the baby because it wouldn't survive. They'd kept Maya on ventilators for a week before she succumbed to her injuries and passed away just shy of six months when their son could have survived.

It had broken Noah's heart to lose them both, and he had yet to recover. He wondered if he would ever love another woman again.

2

Packing her suitcase inside her brownstone on Sunday, Kenya had mixed reservations about meeting her twin at the Canyon Ranch spa. On countless occasions, she'd been there, done that with Chynna, planning something that would fall-through.

Ever since they were little, Chynna had always outshone her. Even when they were born, Kenya had come first, easy breezy for their mother. Then Chynna, as always, had to make a special entrance and come out breach, causing much anxiety for their parents and the doctor. It had been touch-and-go for a moment, and the doctors hadn't been sure they could save Chynna, but out she'd finally come, stealing Kenya's thunder even as a baby. Her parents had forgotten all about their eldest girl because she was coddled comfortably in a blanket by the nurse. They had focused their attention on the wailing new baby girl who *demanded* their attention. And that had just been the beginning.

When they were babies and toddlers, Chynna had always wanted to be the center of everything. She'd cry longer and louder than Kenya, who, according to their mother, would eventually cry herself to sleep, but not Chynna. She would cry until their mother had no choice but to pick up her screaming infant if only to pacify her. And so Kenya's life of being in Chynna's shadow had started.

It had been subtle at first. Chynna refused to be dressed in the same outfit as Kenya, determined to carve out an identity for herself even then. Later, as they grew up, it had become more apparent, especially when their father had left their mother for another woman. Their mother had been devastated, but she'd rose above it to ensure Kenya and Chynna always had a roof over their heads and clothes on their backs. And well, when Chynna wanted signing lessons, she got them. Whatever Chynna wanted, she got. The only time Kenya had asked for anything was when she'd realized she'd had a knack for acting. Becoming someone else had been an escape for her. She could forget being ignored by all the boys who loved Chynna and never seemed to pay any attention to her even though they shared the same face.

Acting was a respite from feeling undervalued. Being in school plays had allowed Kenya to be in the spotlight for the first time in her life. *Why?* Because as luck would have it, Chynna was a gifted singer. She had the voice of an angel and didn't waste an opportunity to be seen *or* heard. Kenya, meanwhile, toiled at her craft, going to NYU and studying acting. Her mother had hated to see Kenya go, but she was too focused on going on the road with Chynna to mind Kenya much.

At NYU, Kenya had flourished, finally coming out of Chynna's shadow to see herself as she was: a damned good actress and wouldn't you know it, a good singer too. No one knew that she could hold a note, much less belt out a song, but it wasn't Kenya's true calling. Instead, she'd worked on getting bit parts in Off-Broadway shows, then Broadway itself, until an agent who said she was made for television had discovered her. Kenya had preferred the quirkiness of New York to the superficiality of L.A., but her agent had insisted she try out for several pilots. It took a year and then some, but after toiling as a waitress, she'd finally managed to land a spot on a great cable TV series which just so happened to shoot in New York, her favorite place.

It was the best of both worlds for Kenya. She would finally be able to do what she loved and get paid for it. The press on their show had been phenomenal, and she'd received rave reviews for her role over the last two years; but the show languished in the bottom of the ratings. Kenya wasn't sure how long the show would go on, but she would keep trying.

A buzzing doorbell awoke Kenya out of her reverie. She rushed over to press down on the intercom button. "Hello?"

"You called for a limo?" a masculine voice said on the other end.

"Be right down." Of course Chynna had arranged for her to travel in style. Kenya should have expected nothing less.

Kenya walked on top of her overstuffed suitcase and snapped it shut. She sure hoped she had enough clothes, but even if she didn't, knowing Chynna, shopping would be inevitable.

She grabbed her suitcase handle, her over-sized carry-on purse that held her magazines, her iPad, and the script of her next episodes she would film after the winter hiatus, and then headed toward the door. "See you soon," she said to her eclectic apartment in downtown SoHo as she turned off the lights.

. . .

WHEN KENYA ARRIVED IN ARIZONA, she was surprised at how alert she was, given the seven-hour flight and connection between New York and Tucson International Airport. But then again, she'd sat in first class both ways, in an oversized, reclining seat, watched a movie, and had as many glasses of Chardonnay that she could possibly drink, thanks to the over-attentive stewardess. This was the best part of meeting Chynna: She always made sure Kenya flew first class.

Exiting the terminal after finding her luggage at baggage claim, she found a liveried driver holding a sign that read "JAMES." *Must be me*, she thought and headed in his direction.

"Kenya James?" he asked when she approached.

"One in the same."

"Great!" He reached for her luggage. "Follow me."

He led her out of the automatic doors into the beautiful sunshine and eighty-five-degree Tucson air. Coming from New York's frigid forty-degree weather was quite a change for Kenya, and she reached into her purse to pull on the enormous Prada shades she'd treated herself too like the other Hollywood celebrities. She followed the driver to a limo waiting at the curb for her and slid in.

She was greeted with "Twinie!"

Kenya smiled as she saw her wayward twin dressed in a designer outfit. "Chynna!" She reached for her sister and gave her a long hug. After their embrace, Kenya sat back to look at her sister. Chynna still looked the same overall, but dark circles under her eyes were telltale signs of lack of sleep.

"It's so good to see a friendly face," Chynna said.

"The last week must have been hell for you," Kenya acknowledged.

"You have no idea." Chynna reached across Kenya for the Dom Perignon that was in the center console in a bucket of ice. She grasped one flute, poured generously and handed it to Kenya before filling one for herself.

Kenya chuckled as she accepted it. Of course, Chynna assumed she was ready to drink champagne at eleven a.m., because that's how you rolled in Chynna's world. "Thanks."

Chynna settled back into the plush leather seat of the limo and took a generous sip before looking back at Kenya. "The press are monsters. I never realized it before. They'd always been good to me."

"Those people are not your friends, Chynna," Kenya responded evenly. "You shouldn't trust the lot of them."

"I know that," Chynna said. "But I've never had them turn on me like this before. They are relentless, showing up everywhere I go, pressing me for information about this supposed affair with Blake. I never even had sex with the man! And now I might as well have a scarlet letter across my chest for all the good my protestations are."

"Well, that's why I'm here," Kenya said, smiling, "to help you get away from it all and have some peace. We'll come up with a strategy to get you out of this mess."

Chynna laughed bitterly. "Probably not one that my label or my manager or my publicist will like."

"True," Kenya surmised. "But whose life is this? Yours or theirs?"

Chynna turned to stare at Kenya for a moment, as

if hearing her for the first time since she'd gotten into the limo. "Mine, of course."

"Then act like it," Kenya said sternly. "Stop letting them walk all over you."

"What do you mean?"

Kenya turned to stare at her incredulously. She remembered how upset Chynna had been about recording her second album—that it had strayed from the sound of her first, but she'd given in to their demands. "Remember how you felt with your second album? Heck, your third?!"

A frown spread across Chynna's face. "Of course," she said testily. "Why are you bringing this up now?"

"Because your label doesn't always have what's best for you in mind, only what's going to make them lots of money."

"I can believe that about most of them, but not Lucas," Chynna said sullenly, folding her arms across her chest. "I believe he genuinely cares about me."

"Is this the same Lucas you've been mooning over and who hasn't paid you one iota of attention?"

"He's just playing hard to get," Chynna fought back.

Kenya shrugged.

"It's easy for you to judge," Chynna replied. "You're not living in my shoes, but I promise you, if you walked a day in my Manolo Blahniks, you'd see it's not so easy being Chynna James."

THEY ARRIVED at Canyon Ranch forty minutes later, but Kenya noticed as they drove along the stone path and tree-lined driveway that they were passing the clubhouse and what appeared to be hotel rooms. Several minutes later, the limo stopped in front of a free-standing home. She stared at Chynna.

"You didn't think we were staying with the common folk?" Chynna inquired. "Not after what I've been through."

Kenya stared open-mouthed as the driver opened the door on Chynna's side and she bounded out of the vehicle. Seconds later, he was at her door and helping her out of the limo. "Thank you."

"You're welcome, ma'am." He walked to the rear of the limo to procure their bags just as a beautiful petite brunette came from the home with a clipboard in hand.

"Welcome, Ms. James," the woman gushed. "We're excited to have you here."

"I'm thankful for the time away," Chynna returned. "And my *privacy*."

"Of course." The woman's hand touched her chest. "Your manager indicated the need for complete anonymity while you're here. The house staff, trainers and chefs we've arranged for you have all signed nondisclosure agreements."

"Excellent!" Chynna sashayed past the woman toward the front door without waiting to see if the woman and Kenya were following.

Kenya felt like a member of Chynna's entourage and followed her inside.

The woman ran in her pumps alongside Chynna. "Casa Grande is at your disposal for the next two weeks," the brunette said. "Casa Grande is twenty-seven hundred square feet and," she continued as they walked inside the foyer, "features a living and dining room, full kitchen, several bedrooms and a private patio."

"We couldn't ask for anything more," Chynna said,

plopping down on the plush suede sofa in the living room.

"Would you like a tour of the home?" the brunette asked.

Kenya glanced down at Chynna, who was already on her iPhone checking her Facebook page or tweeting about something or another. "I would love one." Kenya followed the woman around the home, admiring the beautiful wood ceiling tresses and hardwood floors. The home was done in warm browns and beiges, with pops of color throughout. Kenya was going to enjoy her stay here.

"We have arranged to have a chef cook all of your meals, three times a day, but of course, if *you,*" the brunette said, looking at Kenya, "would like to dine at the clubhouse, then by all means, join us."

Kenya understood the underlying meaning that since she wasn't the celebrity, no one would disturb her; but in the last few weeks, many people had gotten the two of them confused. "Thanks."

After the short tour, they returned to find Chynna on her phone, pacing the living room. Kenya could only assume she was talking to her manager.

"Is there anything else you need?" the brunette inquired, but Chynna waved her off with her hand and headed outside to the private patio.

"That will be all, thank you."

Kenya couldn't believe how rude Chynna was being, but then again, couldn't she? This was who Chynna was at times—an arrogant, self-centered and spoiled diva.

The brunette nodded before leaving the room.

When Chynna returned, she was scowling.

"What's wrong?" Kenya asked.

"Deacon is insisting I should have my bodyguards here, just in case."

Kenya pointed to the door the concierge had just left from. "You heard the woman. They've got this place on lockdown. You've nothing to fear."

Chynna shrugged. "Don't be mad. He says it's for the best."

"Is there no escaping your life?" Kenya inquired and went in search of her luggage that was still sitting in the foyer. She'd already decided on which room she wanted. It was the one that would get the morning sun, which, being a morning person was perfect for Kenya. She would go out for a long run or hike to clear her mind.

"Kenya!" Chynna yelled at her retreating figure; but she was already gone.

WHEN KENYA RETURNED from her run, Chynna was waiting for her.

"I don't want to get into it," Kenya said, heading for her room.

"Well then, you won't hear me say that there will be no bodyguards."

"What?" Kenya turned around.

"I ordered Deacon to call them off," Chynna said proudly. "It will be just us."

A smile rippled across her sister's mouth. "Good for you. I'm going to go shower, and then I'll be ready for lunch."

A half-hour later, the sisters shared a healthy lunch of grilled chicken and a pear, pecan and cranberry salad. Then they went to the spa for a much-needed massage and facial treatment. Afterward, they returned to their villa and sat outside on the patio to watch the sunset with a cup of tea to catch up on old times.

Chynna would have preferred something stronger, but apparently Canyon Ranch was dry unless you brought your own goodies. "I can't believe I escaped to Tucson with no press on my heels."

"Oh, yeah." Kenya sipped on her sparkling water. "Was the press on your tail?"

"You know it," Chynna snapped. "We had to send two decoys in my place to two different locations to throw their scent off."

Kenya sighed and laughed. "Such covert intrigue. Is it always like that? How do you live with it?"

Chynna was silent for a moment as she thought over the question. "On the one hand, I love it. I was born to be a star, but ..."

"But what?"

"But sometimes I wonder what it would be like to be a regular person ... to be able to go to the grocery store on my own without the paparazzi shadowing my every move and trying to catch me without my makeup on."

"It sounds exhausting," Kenya replied.

"It is sometimes. But enough about me. What's going on with you?"

Kenya was shocked that Chynna could manage to turn the conversation away from herself. "Everything's fine."

"Are you sure?" Chynna eyed her suspiciously. "I thought I heard rumors your show could be canceled."

"I sure hope not," Kenya said. "I was reading the next couple of scripts on the plane, and they're writing some brilliant stuff, Emmy-worthy material."

"Ya think?"

Secretly, Kenya had hoped she would've won last year when she'd received an Emmy nod for best dramatic actress, but the Academy had awarded pretty much the same actresses as it had previously, leaving Kenya without a statuette. Everyone had said it was a travesty, and Kenya had tried to put on a brave face, but it hurt always being the bridesmaid and never the bride.

"Well, you're going to win it next time!" Chynna said passionately. "You're a phenomenal actress, Kenya. Always have been. I wish I could say the same."

Ah, and in true form, the conversation returned back to Chynna, Kenya thought.

"Having a hard time with the movie?" Kenya inquired.

"Hard time?" Chynna laughed bitterly. "Make that *worst time.* I'm terrible, and no one is willing to tell me so. They all want me to be this incredible brand of music, movies, perfume, clothes, and usually I'm up for it, but *acting* ...this might be the one thing that's out of my element."

Kenya got a smug feeling inside knowing there was *one* thing she was good at that Chynna couldn't master. "Give it time."

"How much?" Chynna asked, ringing her hands. "If I don't pull it together quick, the director will replace me. Do you think perhaps while we're here, you could run lines with me?"

"Sure." Kenya wasn't sure what good it would be, but she would give it the old college try.

After nearly an hour, Kenya surmised that Chynna just didn't have *it.* That *it* that directors looked for, but she supposed that with a whole lot of editing, the movie studio would figure out how to make it work.

"I'm bad, aren't I?" Chynna asked.

Kenya tried to hide her frustration over Chynna's inability to really let herself *go there.* "You need to be more vulnerable," she stated.

"I'm trying," Chynna responded fervently.

"Well, it's not translating to me," Kenya said. She'd run lines before, but never so painstakingly.

Chynna huffed and stood up. "I'm not into this acting thing. I just want to sing and maybe design an outfit or fragrance, but acting, quite frankly, bores me."

"Then you should never have let them talk you into it. Where's the bullheaded Chynna I know and grew up with? Where has she gone?"

Chynna stared out at the fading sunset and then turned around. "Honestly, I don't know."

"Perhaps it's time you find her."

"And how would I do that?"

Kenya pondered the question. "I don't know, but something's gotta give."

3

Chynna couldn't remember the last time she'd felt truly relaxed and in control of her own destiny than she did over the last week and a half. No schedules, no meetings, no tapings, no concerts. She'd woken up when she wanted, no matter the time of day. She was sure Kenya thought she was crazy sleeping half her morning away over the last week, but she didn't care—she needed to catch up on her sleep.

Between the concerts and the late nights afterward, she was usually up all night and only able to sleep a few hours during the day. Since she'd been at the resort, she went to bed at midnight and got up at nine or ten o'clock, which was quite early for her.

Her twin, on the other hand, was usually already up, had gone for an hour-long run, showered and was sitting at the breakfast table eating an egg-white omelet the chef had prepared. They'd both been blessed with baby-making hips and each had to run or, in Chynna's case, work with a trainer to keep their bodies tight. And tight hers had to remain. Eli was always telling her the camera put on fifteen pounds and that she had to stay within her target weight. Not so easy to do when she was on the road, eating fast food and not getting enough sleep.

She felt better mentally and physically this week than she ever had. She and Kenya had done yoga, Pilates and Zumba. She'd had a massage and facial just about every day, and her pores and skin never seemed so clear. Despite Deacon's protestations, coming to the ranch was a gift.

"Hey, sis," Chynna said, walking into the dining room where Kenya was seated and finishing her omelet.

"Can I have another one of those?" Chynna asked the patient chef, who always waited for her to wake up before starting her breakfast. "But make mine with smoked Gouda, spinach, sautéed mushrooms, onions and some bacon crumbles."

Kenya laughed as she placed another forkful of omelet into her mouth. "You had me until the bacon crumbles."

"Hey, bacon makes everything taste better," Chynna said, plopping in the cushioned chair beside Kenya and folding one leg underneath the other.

"Sure thing," the chef said and busied himself with making her order.

"So what are we going to do today?" Kenya asked.

"I thought we could venture out into the city," Chynna said. "I love the ranch, but I'm dying to see what shopping Tucson has to offer."

"Do you think that's wise? The press has no idea where you are. Why give them any hints?"

"True." The decoys they'd used had worked marvelously and the best the press could come up with was Chynna James had gone into hiding because she was ashamed at having been caught having an affair with a married man. "But as much as I love all this clean living, I need a little retail therapy. Don't deny me one of the few things that make me happy in life."

"It's your funeral," Kenya responded, getting up with her plate and taking it to the kitchen island. She started to rinse it off, but Chef Antoine stopped her.

"Don't worry. I'll take care of it, mon chèri."

"Thank you." She turned to rejoin Chynna.

Chynna was wearing a pouty frown, but then she saw Kenya's stiff shoulders soften. "You'll see, it'll be a lot of fun, and I'll have the concierge call ahead and arrange a few places and we'll go through the back entrance."

SEVERAL HOURS LATER, Chynna pranced in front of the three-way mirror in a sequin, feather mini-dress. High-gloss sequins were sprinkled over a sweetheart neckline, with the feathers dangling and barely reaching her thighs.

"What do you think?" Chynna asked, turning to Kenya, who was seated on the couch outside the dressing room.

"That it barely covers your crotch," Kenya stated honestly.

Chynna rolled her eyes and turned back to the mirror to check out her side view. "This look is in, Kenya. It's hot!"

"If you say so."

Chynna turned back around with a malevolent look in her eye. "It's about high time we got you out of your shell. You have a body as good, *no,* better than mine, and you can flaunt it."

She looked over at the store attendant who'd been

graciously helping them. As soon as they'd entered the exclusive boutique, she'd made it clear she was used to celebrities frequenting the store and that Chynna needn't worry about any disturbances because she'd closed down the store. Chynna had hoped that would be the case and had informed the attendant she would be spending an outrageous sum of money, which had brought a smile from the store owner.

"Can you please get my twin here the sexiest dress you can find, and she'll try it own and *I'll* buy it."

"Absolutely, Ms. James." The store owner departed the fitting area.

"I don't need to try on that stuff," Kenya protested. "It's not me."

"How would you know? You live in your bubble in New York."

"Ouch." Kenya frowned.

"I'm sorry," Chynna apologized, but it wasn't quite sincere. Kenya needed to live a little. "When was your last date?"

Kenya shrugged. "I don't know ... a few months ago, maybe six. What does that have to do with anything?"

"It means you've fallen off the horse and you have to get back on."

"I just haven't found the right man who excites me. I want a strong, take-charge man. A real man's man. One who isn't afraid to get dirty and maybe change a flat tire and ruin his manicure."

"A man not into all the Hollywood bullshit?"

"You feel me." Kenya pointed back to Chynna.

"That describes Lucas Kingston," Chynna said, "in a nutshell."

"Huph," Kenya huffed.

"Hey, hey." Chynna shook her finger at Kenya. "Don't talk about *my man* like that."

Kenya chuckled. "Does he know he's your man?"

"Soon," Chynna promised. "Real soon."

"YOU'RE TELLING me Chynna still isn't back yet from this week-long sabbatical?" Lucas asked Deacon later that evening.

Deacon hated when the man turned the midnight eyes on him. Wasn't it enough that he was six foot five, built like a running back, and outweighed him by a hundred pounds? Did he have to have piercing eyes too? "No, she's not back yet."

Lucas slammed his fists on his desk. "We've already canceled two tour dates because of all this foolishness with Blake Cooper. She needs to get her butt back here."

"She's not ready yet."

"Not ready?" Lucas said. "It's been over a week and the salaciousness of this story isn't dying down. She needs to face the press. If she doesn't, she'll always be in fear of them. Sometimes you have to look a bully in the face. You know what I'm saying?"

"I don't disagree, Lucas," Deacon responded. "And I tried to tell her as much, but after she talked to her twin, she was convinced it was in her best interest."

"Oh, that's right," Lucas said. "She has a twin—an identical one, right?"

Deacon nodded.

"Have you ever met her?"

"Couple of times, but not for long. Kenya hates the L.A. scene and Chynna usually goes out there to her or meets her somewhere else. In her own words, 'I want to keep my family life private,' which makes this thing with Blake so crazy. Sure, she's an incorrigible flirt, but she'd never do anything reckless."

Lucas shook his head in agreement. *Incorrigible* flirt was correct. Chynna James had set her sights on him and was always trying to get his attention, but he, like this twin of hers, wasn't interested in the L.A. sun either. Surprising given that he'd gone into business with his best friend, Eli Ross, to start R&K Records, but then again, he was supposed to be a silent partner. Eli was supposed to be the face because the man could spot talent in a heartbeat. But when Eli's mismanagement became apparent, Lucas had to step in and forgo being hidden in the shadows or risk losing his investment. So, Lucas had gotten sucked into the game, much to his own dismay. Eli continued to handle talent, but Lucas kept his eyes on everything now, and Chynna sashaying her butt out of town was costing him money and he didn't like it one bit.

"Where is she?" Lucas rose from his seat and walked over to stand in front of Deacon. He knew his basketball player height scared the manager, but he wasn't above using intimidation to get his way. He needed Chynna back *now*.

"No can do, Lucas," Deacon said. "Chynna's been my client for years, and I can't go against her wishes."

"But you don't mind getting those bonuses from the record label either."

Deacon began slowly backing away from Lucas and heading toward the door. "I don't mind them a bit, but Chynna would have my head and I can't betray her."

"Well, you tell your client she'd better have her butt back here and ready to fight before her third concert on Friday. If I have to cancel another, it'll be coming out of her pocket. Capish?"

Deacon reached the door in record time and turned the handle. "I'll be sure to relay your message to Chynna."

Seconds later, the short, bald man was out of Lucas's office, and he sighed heavily.

Why does Chynna have to be so contrary? If he didn't need her so much, he'd throttle her. Somehow, someway, he'd get Chynna James back on course, and he would use any method necessary.

She reminded him of his little sister living in South Central. She'd gone the wrong way and had ended up pregnant with three kids. And as much as he loved his niece and nephews, his sister didn't need to have babies at sixteen. If only she hadn't been in such a hurry to grow up and experience life so fast.

That's who Chynna reminded him of. She'd gotten in this business too young, and in order to be seen and heard, she always had to be the center of attention, and what better way than by being contrary? *Doesn't she realize there are consequences to her actions?* The world didn't just stop because Chynna decided she needed a break from reality.

Life hadn't been easy for Lucas either. He'd had to work for everything he'd ever obtained. He'd started out in the rough and tough streets of South Central. It would've been easy for him to fall the way of a lot of young black men to drugs and violence. But Lucas had other plans: to get the hell out of South Central as fast as his body and mind could get him. Excelling at school and getting a scholarship to UCLA had been high on his list of priorities, and he'd done just that. And now, he wasn't about to let some spoiled pop star ruin what it had taken him so long to gain.

When Chynna came back to L.A., he was going to have a come- to-Jesus moment with the starlet and tell her in no uncertain terms that he wouldn't put up with her bullshit, no matter how much she was adored my millions of fans.

4

After a long, strenuous hike, Kenya returned to their villa to find Chynna at the baby grand piano with a pen and paper in hand and singing softly. The melody was beautiful, and Kenya couldn't resist saying as much. "That's really pretty, twinie."

Chynna turned around. "You think so? It's something new I've been working on since we've been here."

"It's really good," Kenya commented. "Reminds me of your first album."

Chynna nodded. "Yeah, I doubt the label would be happy with it. What's hot right now is up-tempo beats with synthesizers."

"Just because it's hot doesn't mean you have to follow the trend. It's okay to be different. Unique. Special. Isn't that what Mama always said?" asked Kenya, approaching her sister.

She saw Chynna's shoulders instantly stiffen in response at mentioning their deceased mother. She knew it was hard for Chynna to think about her, knowing that no amount of money in the world could've saved her. Their mother had always been the picture of health or so they'd thought. They hadn't known she was taking blood pressure pills to regulate her hypertension. How could they have known she couldn't afford them and wasn't taking them, and that it would cause her to suddenly keel over and die unexpectedly at fifty years old? It had been a shock to both of them.

Kenya wondered if that's when they'd drifted apart, each living in different parts of the country because they hadn't done a better job at watching over the only parent who cared about them. Their father had only reemerged after Chynna's success, and neither she nor Kenya had been interested. They'd felt it was especially hypocritical when he'd called to give his condolences and requested to come to the funeral. Truth be told, Kenya had always felt like her mother had never recovered from his betrayal and had died of a broken heart.

"I'm sorry Chy—," she began, but Chynna pulled away. Kenya pursued her train of thought. "I know it was hard losing Mama, Chynna, but we're all we've got."

"Really?" Chynna asked. "Is that why you stay in New York and never visit? Is that why I only see you when I'm in town or twist your arm to meet me someplace?"

Kenya was shocked by Chynna's outburst and gave a nervous laugh. "You know how much I hate L.A."

"Bullshit!" Chynna stood up. "You and both know what this is about."

Kenya folded her arms across her chest. "And what's it about?"

"I know everyone thinks I'm a ditzy airhead that has to be told what to do, what to sing and how to dress, but I have two eyes, Kenya. I know you're jealous of me and all I have, and that's why you won't come around me. Do you hate me that much?"

Tears sprung to Kenya's eyes. Chynna had struck a nerve. Yes, she'd felt envy because she'd always felt second best or less than, but hate? "Hate?" She shook her head. "I could never hate you. You're my twin. Hating you would be like hating myself."

"Then perhaps you hate yourself. Maybe that's why you keep me at arm's length."

The words pierced Kenya's heart as if she'd been stabbed, and she staggered away from Chynna and toward the sofa. She sank into the plushness and buried her head in her hands and started sobbing. Had they really come to this—accusing each other of such horrible things?

Chynna must have realized just how deeply she'd cut Kenya, because she rushed to Kenya's side and fell to her knees, grasping Kenya's hands.

All Kenya could do was stare blankly at her as hot tears fell down her cheeks. She'd never felt so raw, so exposed. "Is that really how you see me?"

"Sometimes," Chynna admitted, sinking down onto her haunches besides Kenya. "Do you think it's so easy being me? Constantly living in front of the camera? Having my every move scrutinized, analyzed, commented on?"

Kenya sat forward. "But you love and eat it up with a spoon."

"Do I?" Chynna asked, looking into her brown eyes. "Or is that the persona I've created that now even you don't know the real me? C'mon, twinie, look into my eyes."

Kenya stared at Chynna in disbelief. Was she really so off the mark on her own twin? They used to be able to read each other's thoughts, know what the other would say before they said it. But now, since Mama's death and Chynna's rise to fame, they'd grown apart and Kenya wasn't so sure. She slid down the sofa to sit beside Chynna on the carpet.

Chynna leaned her back against the sofa and said, "Do you know how much I've enjoyed the peace and the quiet here at the ranch this week? I don't have a moment of peace in my everyday life. I'm constantly going from one meeting to another, never having any privacy. So yes, I put up a front that I'm having the time of my life when, in fact, I would like to be curled up with a good book instead of on a red carpet, movie premiere or club- hopping."

Kenya gave her a sideward glance. "I never knew."

"Because you never asked. You just assumed that it's all fun and games. You should come live in my shoes and see what it's like to be me, and then you'd see."

"I can only imagine."

Chynna sat upright in her seat. "Oh, my gosh! That's it!"

Kenya stared at her blankly. "That's what?"

Chynna's eyes were bright with devilry when she said with a straight face, "We should switch places."

"Say what?"

"You heard me."

Kenya chuckled at the thought. "We haven't switched places in years." She remembered when they were little and they used to confuse their mother, but eventually she had been able to tell them apart. But most of their friends couldn't and Chynna and Kenya took great pleasure in throwing them off.

"So, it could still work."

Kenya shook her head. "We're too different."

"But not in looks," Chynna said and gave Kenya's

body a frank assessment. "You're in great shape, just like me. And the face, well, the differences have always been subtle to most people. They'll never be able to tell. The only thing we need to do is give you some honey-blond highlights and you're set."

"Are you seriously thinking about this?" Kenya asked incredulously, touching her shoulder-length dark-brown hair.

"Hell yes!"

"Why?"

"I need a break from my life and the press for a while," Chynna said. "And you've always wondered what it would like to be me, envied it. Well, here's your chance. You'd get to be me for a week or so while I soak in more peace and quiet and crank out an album that I'll actually love singing."

Chynna noticed how quiet Kenya was being. She was giving what Chynna was saying serious credence. Chynna knew Kenya wanted to do it, but she needed the final push.

"And what would I get out of this?"

"You'll get the greatest acting opportunity of your life: portraying me."

"You think I can play you?"

A soft, loving curve touched Chynna's lips. "I know you can. You're an amazing actress and quite frankly, you'll probably wow them during the filming of the movie."

"Oh!" Kenya's hand went to her mouth, and Chynna knew she'd found her icing on the cake.

"Think about it. You'd get to act in a motion picture."

"Yeah, but I would be playing you playing someone else."

"And? Are you saying you're not up to the task? To

pull off the biggest double cross ever? I know you can sing, Kenya."

"What?" Kenya pretended to play dumb.

"Don't act like you don't know what I'm talking about. I saw you sing on Broadway."

"When did you see me?"

"I had an unexpected stop in New York and heard about this great Broadway show that was getting a lot of buzz, so I decided to check it out. Imagine my surprise to see my sister on stage with the voice of a nightingale. Not to mention I watch your show."

"You do? Why didn't you say anything?"

"Because I figured singing was a gift you wanted to keep hidden. Here, everyone was touting me as the songstress when in fact, it runs in the family. So I know you can do this."

"Even if I agreed to this," Kenya replied, "why would you? Why would you allow me to live your life?"

"I think you're right," Chynna stated. "I've lost my way, and I've let other people make decisions for me. I guess after Mama passed after my first album, it seemed easier to let someone else deal with everything. I have to figure out who I am without any interruptions. And what better place than this oasis?"

Kenya's eyes grew large with excitement, but Chynna could see she was still wrapping her head around the idea. "This is crazy."

"Maybe, but totally doable. Listen, I'm not asking you to do it long-term. Just for a week or so until I get my head on straight and remember who the real Chynna is."

"I'm gonna need to sleep on this."

"And tomorrow, you'll see this is the best idea I've ever had."

. . .

KENYA AWOKE the next morning after a fitful night of tossing and turning. Even with the dawn of a new day, she was still wrestling with whether she should consider Chynna's harebrained scheme. *Should I go for it and walk in Chynna's high-heeled shoes?*

She didn't have anything pressing coming up. Her show was on winter hiatus, and it would be sort of fun to act like her outrageous sister for a change. But there were so many variables to consider. She would not only have to act like Chynna, she would have to *become* her. She would have to sing in front of thousands at her next tour stop, go to movie rehearsals, and hadn't Chynna mentioned the taping of a video coming up? Not to mention convincing Chynna's entire entourage, manager, publicist and record label that she was the real deal. Hmm ... she could be biting off more than she could chew.

A knock sounded on her bedroom door, and Kenya sat up in her bed. "Come in."

Chynna's head popped through the corner of the door. "You up?"

"Yeah," Kenya said. "I am. Been thinking about this crazy scheme of yours."

"And what have you decided?"

"That it could work. But your life is so hectic and I don't know ..." Her voice trailed off.

"I can give you a twelve-hour crash course in how to be Chynna James, and you'll be right as rain to get on a plane tomorrow."

"Tomorrow?" Kenya's voice rose.

"Yes, I received a call from Deacon last night that Lucas ordered me to get my butt back to L.A. and that he couldn't cancel any more concerts."

"I don't know, Chynna. That's not enough time to prepare." Usually she had weeks to study her characters, understand their flaws and give a nuanced performance.

"You've had to learn lines before in a hurry, haven't you?" Chynna said. "This is no different."

"Like hell it isn't." Kenya threw back the covers and slid from between the sheets to rise to her feet. "You have people around you all the time. How am I supposed to convince them I'm you?"

Chynna walked toward Kenya. "It's really not that difficult. Act like you don't care. Be easy breezy. Go with the flow."

"That's easier said than done." Kenya wasn't like Chynna at all. She was driven and focused and knew what she was doing and when. It would require all of her acting skills to act footloose and fancy-free.

"We can do this, starting now." Chynna grabbed Kenya by the hand.

ON THEIR WAY to the hair salon to get Kenya some blond highlights, Chynna went through everyone in her entourage with Kenya, starting with Deacon and telling her how they'd met and how Chynna had instantly disliked him because he'd called her unsophisticated and in need of polish. She filled Kenya in on Fiona and her penchant for Louboutins and Brighton, and sweet Penelope, who could use some encouragement in the confidence department. She told her about Eric, one of her dancers with whom she'd shared a one-night stand after a few too many shots of Patrón on South Beach.

Later that evening in Chynna's room, she walked Kenya through her wardrobe and what she would wear to hang out, go to the club or wear on stage. Kenya wouldn't be caught dead in the flashy, sparkly, tight-fitting clothes that Chynna wore.

"Try this one." Chynna held up some snug skinny jeans and a spaghetti strap plunge top.

Kenya frowned with distaste, but slipped out of her pajamas to try on the garments. "Totally not my style."

"Well, you're going to have to learn to love it," Chynna said, "because it's yours for the next week."

After she slid the jeans over her curvy hips and pulled the sparkling top down, Kenya turned around to stare at her reflection in the mirror. She was surprised to see that she actually looked quite hot in Chynna's clothes.

"See? I told you," Chynna said as Kenya continued to stare at herself in the mirror. "You don't know how sexy you truly are."

Kenya spun around to admire her behind in the skinny jeans.

"Now that you have the clothes," Chynna said, "you need the attitude and walk to go with it." She stood up to demonstrate her infamous walk that to Kenya looked like a fashion model's walk on the runway.

"When you're at an event, don't look anyone in the face," Chynna said, looking straight ahead as she walked. "Look beyond them as if what you're about to do it is ten times more important."

"And is it?"

Chynna laughed. "Usually, but not always." She stopped suddenly and turned around to face Kenya. "Listen, you're a diva. Or that's what people think of me. Act like it. Never pour your own drink or pull out your own chair. Let someone else do that for you."

"I don't know if I can get used to being waited on hand and foot. I'm used to doing for myself. I'm an independent woman."

"Well, in *my world*," Chynna emphasized, "you have people to do that for you. Derrick is your hair stylist. He will hook up any style or weave you want. He's a talker, always wanting to talk about what straight man he's turned gay, so be ready to listen. Daisy is my makeup artist, a loud Goth girl, who I can't quite understand why she hangs out with our bunch because she likes heavy metal music, but she makes me, *now you,* look fabulous. Then there's Megan. She's my wardrobe stylist. Let her pick out things for you. Don't be afraid to try on her crazy ideas, because they'll usually come together in surprising ways."

Kenya was exhausted just listening to all the people who were in Chynna's orbit and fluttered around her every day. *How does she live with the excess?* "Anything else?"

"Well, that brings me to my upcoming music video."

"Oh Lord!" Kenya rolled her eyes upward. She'd never been much of a dancer and doubted now would be any different. There was no way she was going to learn all of Chynna's routines in, she glanced at her watch, six hours.

"You're going to have to fake it till you make it," Chynna replied. "I'm going to show you some of my basic moves and you're just going to have wing it. Worst case, my male dancers will come in and help you out. Follow their lead."

Kenya stared at her incredulously. "Chynna, you're a great dancer and I'm not. Yes, I can sing and I know all your songs by heart, but dancing? This is a stretch."

Chynna ignored Kenya's protestations and went over the docking station that housed her iPod. She swirled her thumb around until she came to one of her more energetic songs and turned up the music. "Alright, Kenya, show me what you're working with."

HOURS LATER, sweaty and hungry, Kenya watched the chef make what would be her final meal with her sister for the imminent future. Deacon had arranged for Chynna's plane to come to Tucson and a car would be sent the next morning to fetch her, *Kenya* that was.

Am I really ready for this? Sure, she'd said she could do it. But after a few hours of practicing Chynna's major routines and prancing around in her five-inch heels and sexy outfits, Kenya was exhausted. Imitation was supposed to be the sincerest form of flattery, but Kenya wasn't sure she could pull it off.

"I know this seems daunting," Chynna said, coming to sit beside her, "but I have absolute faith in you."

"Yeah, because it'll be my butt out there singing and dancing onstage every night while you're here relaxing and having massages and facials."

"You don't know how, how much this means to me, Kenya." Chynna's voice broke when she spoke. "I've been under so much pressure the last few years to stay on top, to be the best, to stay relevant. I'm at the end of my rope. I just need a little time to myself to remember what it is I truly like about this business."

Kenya frowned. "Are you thinking of retiring and doing a Lauryn Hill?"

Chynna shrugged. "I don't know." When Kenya's eyes grew large like saucers, Chynna rephrased, "I doubt it. I think I'm just burned out. You're taking my place for a while is just what I need. I can't thank you enough, twinie."

Chynna reached for Kenya's hand and gave her a squeeze. "I'm happy I can do this for you. But you know this is only for a short while, and that you'll have to come back to your life."

"I know, I know."

5

Chynna stared out the window of the villa as her sister drove away in the limousine Deacon had sent for her. She felt a little sad and bereft at losing her other half after two weeks together but excited at the prospect of having her life to herself for the next week or more. She knew it was extremely selfish of her to ask Kenya for this gift, and the fact her twin would do this told Chynna of the depth of her love. And that even though their mother was gone, Chynna still had someone left who loved her and remembered her before all the fame and fortune got a hold of her.

This time would be a period of self-discovery for her, a reminder that she was more than just a *brand* and sex symbol. Sometimes, Deacon, Fiona, Lucas and especially Eli forgot she was a real person with real feelings and emotions. They just expected her to get onstage and perform like she was some kind of circus act. Forget that she'd been on tour the better part of the last five years. Forget that she hadn't had a real vacation, other than a few days here and there and an odd weekend with Kenya in New York.

Chynna was looking forward to some much

needed R&R; she was really looking forward to nice long hikes in the mountains. Kenya had been raving about it for the last couple of weeks, but Chynna hadn't been interested in it until now. Now she had plenty of time on her hands to enjoy the sights and sounds without worrying about what was around the corner.

After a quick shower, Chynna put on her khaki shorts, tank top and laced up her tennis shoes and headed for the door for whatever adventure awaited her. She hoped Kenya would enjoy hers too.

BUTTERFLIES SWARMED in the pit of Kenya's stomach as she sat in the back of the limo. When it had arrived at the villa doorstep earlier that morning, she'd thought she'd been prepared. Dressed in one of Chynna's designer outfits complete with miniskirt, big gold hoops, Prada shades and gold stilettos, Kenya looked just like her, but as soon as the doorbell rang, Kenya had thought about dashing.

Even though they hadn't always had the strongest of relationships, she'd promised Chynna she'd do this. Not to mention Chynna was offering her the chance to act out her fantasy of what it would be like to live a day in her sister's shoes. And she wouldn't just live a day. She would live a week. It would be *the* most important acting job of her entire career. *Can I convince everyone in Chynna's life that I'm the real deal?*

She was now finding out, because as she slid inside the limo, she was greeted by a strong masculine hand pulling her inside and down onto the plush leather seat behind him. When she managed to look up at who was manhandling her, she found herself staring into a pair of eyes as dark as midnight and like nothing she'd ever seen. Kenya swallowed hard.

"Thought I'd better come fetch you myself," Lucas Kingston said at Kenya's dumbfounded expression, "in case you tried to make a run for it."

All of Chynna's words went out the window and Kenya snatched her arm away. "I don't care to be man-handled."

"Then don't run off and leave me holding the bag and making apologizes to promoters and your fans," Lucas replied. "I don't find your antics amusing, Chynna. You cost me a lot of money."

"Then perhaps you need to think about giving your slaves a day out of the fields, massa," Kenya drawled.

Lucas's head spun around to face her, surprised by her outburst. He stared at Kenya strangely. *Have I already messed this up?* "Wow! Someone went away for a couple of weeks and got a smart mouth."

Kenya smoothed down her miniskirt, which kept rising up her thigh, much to her consternation, but obviously not to Lucas's because he watched her discomfort and a bemused smile spread across his face. "What's with you, Chynna?" he inquired. "I'd think you'd be hiking that skirt up a bit more for my benefit."

Kenya huffed and looked out the window. *Never look anyone in the face.* "Well, perhaps I got tired of waiting for you to notice."

Lucas laughed and Kenya felt the rich timbre reach her very core. No wonder Chynna had a crush on this man. He was all man and all sex. He was handsome, dark chocolate with close-cut hair and a sexy swagger. He wore a silver pinstriped suit and was the type of man who commanded attention and exuded charisma, but that also made him very arrogant.

"You're full of fire today," Lucas replied. "Makes me curious to find out why."

Kenya turned the full glare of her hazel eyes on Lucas. "In your dreams."

Lucas moved backward to assess her more carefully. "So, it's like that now, huh? Now that I've shown an inkling of an interest, you're no longer into me?"

"Who said I ever was?" Kenya threw back at him. "Perhaps it was all in your head, and I don't mean the one on top of your shoulders."

"Ouch!" Lucas touched his chest as if mortally wounded. "The claws have come out today." He couldn't remember a time when Chynna had acted less interested in him then she was that very moment. He didn't understand it. The woman was a mystery he might be curious to unearth.

"C'mon." Kenya laughed. "I doubt you're all that wounded. You'll have a bevy of beauties surrounding you in L.A. in no time, eager for some time with the top music executive."

"Would that make you jealous?" Lucas asked. He didn't know why he was toying with Chynna when it was obvious she'd moved on from her infatuation with him; he didn't know why that bothered him. Perhaps because today she'd shown fire and hadn't minded telling him where to go instead of acting like a yes-woman as she had of late. Where had this Chynna been?

"Not in the slightest," Kenya said and proceeded to put in the earbuds she'd thankfully remembered to throw into Chynna's oversized Ferragamo tote.

The rest of the ride to the airport was fraught with

silence, and Kenya didn't choose to change it. She needed to keep Lucas Kingston at a distance. It wouldn't do to have him too close and risk him discovering their secret. If he discovered what they were up to, they would go down in flames.

NOAH ROAD the stallion that he'd finally broken after two long weeks along the perimeter of the family's Golden Oaks Ranch. He was the oldest Hart, followed by Rylee. Then there was Caleb, the youngest of his siblings. If you said tomato, he said tomahto. He always had to be contrary. Had been that way since the day he was born. Noah had wanted to strangle the little boy with the smart mouth who followed him everywhere. But there wasn't anything he wouldn't do for his baby brother or Rylee, for that matter. Family meant everything to him.

It's why he'd come back to the ranch after graduation and receiving his degree in Business Administration. He'd wanted to grow the family business from just a cattle ranch, and he had. Golden Oaks was still a working cattle ranch, but it was also a dude ranch where tourists could come to hike, horseback ride, and fish and engage in any other activity that reminded them of days gone by.

Noah disembarked from the horse and tied the reins to the fence. He stared out at the cows grazing in a nearby pasture. He'd hoped to have a family of his own one day, but apparently that hadn't been God's will. And Noah had had a bone to pick with the man upstairs ever since. How could someone as beautiful and kind as Maya be gone and murderers and rapists live long, healthy lives? It just didn't seem fair.

He was so deep in thought he didn't see the Jeep swerve away from one of the cows that had broken free from the pack until the Jeep came speeding toward him. Noah only had moments to loosen the reins and send the horse to safety before tossing himself to the ground to avoid the car that smashed into the ranch's fence.

"What the hell?" Noah swore as he rose from the ground and wiped off the grass from his jeans. Then he noticed the airbag had deployed in the Jeep, and he rushed over to make sure the driver wasn't injured.

Swiftly, he opened the driver's door. The driver was female. Her head was pressed down on the steering wheel, so he gently lifted her head to assess the damage. Her hair was in her face and when he brushed it back to check for cuts and bruises, he was surprised to see the most beautiful woman he'd ever met, save for the swelling bruise on her forehead.

Her eyes flickered open, and he caught the specks of green in their murky depths. She blinked several times, clearly disoriented. "It's okay," he whispered softly. "You crashed, but you're okay."

She glanced around her, unfamiliar with her surroundings, and Noah heard the sweetest voice ever say, "Where am I?"

"On my family's ranch. You crashed into our fence."

"Ah." Chynna shook her head. "Now, I remember. A damn cow came at me and attacked."

Noah chuckled, amused by her word choice. "I highly doubt he attacked you. Cows don't like vehicles. She was just trying to get away from your Jeep."

"Didn't seem that way to me," Chynna said as she unsuccessfully tried to move and disentangle herself from the seatbelt wrapped around her. "Wait a second. Are they yours?"

"Yeah, why?"

"You need to warn your cows about drivers on the road."

"Well, you're the one on private property," he responded evenly.

"Am I?" Chynna asked, scratching her head. "I must have made a wrong turn on the way back to Canyon Ranch."

So she was one of *those* women, Noah surmised. Women who have so much free time on their hands they have to sit around, getting pampered all the time.

"Here, let me help you with that." He leaned over to help unbuckle her seatbelt.

"Thank you," Chynna said, then spun so she could lower her feet to the ground, but when she did, the ground all of sudden began to spin around her, and she clutched the muscled arm of her rescuer.

"Easy," Noah said. "You just hit your head and need to take it easy."

The woman attempted to shake him off, but he had a firm hand on her arm to keep her steady.

"I can take care of myself," she said.

"That's debatable," Noah replied.

Her eyes narrowed at him.

"Why don't you let me take you back to the ranch? We'll get you looked at, and I'll get someone to take care of your vehicle."

"That's really not necessary," she said and wiggled her arm out of his grasp.

"I insist," Noah pressed. "You need to have that bump looked at." He inclined his head to the growing bump at the base of her hairline.

The woman reached up to touch her forehead and a frown formed on her mouth.

"So, what's it going to be?" Noah asked.

"That depends on two things," she replied.

"Oh, yeah? What's that?"

"Well, first, I don't know your name, and second, how are we going to get back to your ranch?" She glanced around and didn't see any vehicles nearby.

Noah offered her his hand. "The name's Noah Hart. My family owns Golden Oaks Ranch. And our mode of transportation is that lovely horse." He pointed to a stallion grazing about a hundred yards away.

The woman pointed to the horse. "You expect me to ride on that?"

"Do you have a better idea? The only other way home is to walk, and I promise you in this eighty-five-degree heat, you don't want to burn that pretty little skin of yours."

He noticed just how fair her café-au-lait skin was and just how smooth. There were no visible marks on her clear skin ... skin that he had an overwhelming desire to touch and see if it was as smooth as it looked.

The woman thought about it for a moment and then said, "I guess I have no choice since your cattle ran me off the road."

Noah laughed at her constantly changing story. "But before I allow some reckless driver to ride my horse, I don't believe I caught your name either."

The woman paused for what seemed like an eternity before giving him her answer. Didn't she know her own name? Or was it that she didn't want to tell him. She finally responded. "Kenya. Kenya James."

"Pleasure to meet you, Kenya," Noah replied. "Stay here. I'll go get Max."

. . .

THE SEXY COWBOY was gone for a few minutes, giving Chynna enough time to collect her wits. *What the hell had just happened?* Had she just told him she was her sister? But what else could she have done? She couldn't exactly tell him who she really was, a runaway pop star trying to find herself. She doubted he would believe her. Then again, did cowboys like him even listen to the Hot 100 on the radio? He probably had no idea who she really was, which wasn't a bad thing. Anyway, she'd told him she was Kenya. She'd made her bed, and now she was going to have to lie in it.

He returned several moments later with the reins of the thoroughbred firmly in his hands—strong, calloused hands from what she could see. These were hands that would know what to do with a horse ... or a woman's body, for that matter.

Now that she wasn't so blurry-eyed from the crash, she could really take her time and assess just how handsome the cowboy was who had rescued her.

Noah Hart was classically handsome with warm brown skin, a strong chin and jaw, closely cut hair, a permanent five o'clock shadow and a disarming smile that when he chose to bestow one caused a warmth to spread through her loins. He was dressed simply in casual jeans and a jean shirt.

"Do I pass inspection?" Noah asked, breaking into her thoughts.

Chynna blinked several times. "What was that?"

Noah motioned to the sky that had turned overcast all of a sudden and was turning darker instantly. "Storm clouds. We need to get a move on if we want to make it to the ranch."

"Do you think we'll make it there in time?" Chynna asked as he gave her a lift onto the back of the horse. He didn't seem to mind, placing his hand on her bottom and hoisting her over.

"Just enough," Noah said as he quickly jumped astride the horse behind Chynna before she had time to object about how close he was to her. Noah grabbed the reins of the horse and took off in a gallop.

"What about the Jeep?" Chynna asked, peering over him to look at the stranded vehicle.

"Don't worry. I'll take care of it," Noah said as his muscled arms surrounded her and led the horse in the direction of what Chynna could only assume was his family's ranch.

Noah was quiet on the twenty-minute ride across the grassland. Chynna noticed that the Hart ranch must be pretty extensive, because they passed tons of cattle and horses grazing, a hay storage facility, stables, a dozen smaller guest cabins and another row of mini-houses she assumed housed the onsite staff.

Unfortunately, they didn't beat the rain, which had started coming down five minutes earlier. By the time Noah guided the horse into the covered stables, Chynna was soaked head to toe.

Noah disembarked first, not caring about his appearance, but Chynna was mortified. She'd left the house wearing nothing but a tank top, shorts and her tennis shoes. She'd never thought to bring a change of clothes, because she'd assumed she'd be back in her villa.

"Okay, princess?" Noah held out his arms to her.

"I'm soaked," Chynna complained from atop the horse.

Mentioning her wet attire, Chynna spurred Noah out of his down-to-business attitude to remember she was a flesh-and-blood woman, and his eyes darted to her breasts, which in her rain-soaked tank top was plastered to her like a second skin. The cold air had caused her nipples to form into tiny buds.

Noah must have sensed her self-consciousness, because he reached for a nearby hook where a suede jacket hung and handed it to her. "For you, my lady."

"How chivalrous of you," Chynna said as she slipped her arms into the warm coat. When she was done, she swung one leg over, and before she knew it, Noah grabbed a hold of her hips to help her solidly to the ground. She turned around to thank him, and his eyes were cloudy with something she couldn't quite detect. Lust. Fear. Anger. There were a lot of emotions running through Noah Hart. But before she could act or question any of them, he'd turned away.

With his back to her, he said, "When the rain lets up, I'll take you back to your spa. In the meantime, you'll have to hang out here. That's if you don't mind slumming it."

At her sharp intake of breath, Noah knew he'd overstepped a boundary.

"Slumming it?" Chynna asked.

"Well, you were at the Canyon Spa, and only rich women with a lot of time on their hands go there."

Chynna folded her arms across her chest. "Oh, really? And what would you know about it?"

"Plenty, actually," Noah replied. "My family has had this ranch for over thirty-five years, and we've seen plenty of folks come and go. Some of those very same rich women came here to our dude ranch thinking it was going to be the same as Canyon Ranch, and they were sorely disappointed that there weren't spa treatments and yoga every day."

"Has anyone ever told you you're judgmental?"

"Many folks have," a female voice said from behind them.

Noah turned around, and a petite female with wild, unruly spiral curls hanging down her back was watching them. She was cute as a button with big brown eyes, curly lashes and a shapely figure. She had the same coloring and facial features as Noah, and Chynna surmised that they must be related.

"No one asked you, Ry," Noah replied.

"Well, I offered." Rylee came forward with a friendly smile as she offered her hand. "Rylee Hart, Noah's sister."

Chynna looked back and forth at the two of them. "I couldn't have guessed."

"Noah seems to think he knows everything from people to horses." Rylee eyed her brother suspiciously.

"I'm usually right," Noah said, walking away from them and removing the bridle, harness and saddle off the horse. He grabbed a brush from the tack room and returned with several biscuit treats that he fed the horse before brushing him down to cool him off.

"You look like you could use a shower," Rylee said, looking at Chynna in her brother's suede jacket and wet clothes.

"Yeah, we kind of got caught in the downpour."

"After Kenya here ploughed her Jeep into our fence," Noah commented, continuing to brush the horse down.

Rylee looked at Chynna strangely when Noah called her Kenya. Did Rylee know who she was? She couldn't have because she said nothing, so Chynna shrugged it off. Clearly, her anxiety was getting the best of her. No one knew her true identity. It wouldn't do for the press to get wind of her whereabouts.

"C'mon, let's get you cleaned up," Rylee said, walking toward the exit of the stables. She grabbed her rain jacket off a nearby hook and wrapped it around her. "We'll see you inside," she told her brother, who merely nodded his assent without a backward glance.

Chynna glanced at his back for several long minutes. She was certain she'd seen something in his eyes before Rylee had appeared. Had she imagined a flicker of interest? Noah Hart was a good-looking, red-blooded male like any other, and she usually knew when a man was interested.

She didn't have time to think about it because Rylee was heading through the stable door. They ran in the downpour past a Zen garden with a wheelbarrow and hammock and into their family home.

"This is the main house," Rylee said, walking up the wooden steps onto the porch. She removed her raincoat and shook it out.

To Chynna, it was far from just a house. From the outside, it was more like an estate, thanks to a second nearby house not far from the main one.

Rylee noticed Chynna looking in that direction. "Oh, that's just the guesthouse."

"What about the cabins I saw earlier?"

"Oh, those are for paying guests. That house is for *our* personal guests," Rylee said as she led her inside the foyer. She hung up her rain jacket on a coat rack near the door.

"Oh." Chynna's mouth dropped when she saw the inside of the home as she removed Noah's jacket. Hardwood floors, stone fireplaces, a grand foyer and staircase, corridors that went on for miles and stuffed deer heads adorned the walls. She handed the rain-soaked jacket to Rylee, who added it to hers on the rack.

"I would offer you a tour," Rylee said, "but I think you'd like a shower first, yes?"

"Would love one."

"Follow me." Rylee led Chynna up the circular staircase that led to the second story of the home, which went in several directions from north to south to east and west. "We'll go to my wing of the house." She led Chynna past several doors on the east side.

They stopped, and Rylee opened the door to what must've been her room because it was ultra-feminine and ultra-glam with a large four-poster canopy bed done in champagne.

Rylee left Chynna to her own devices and went through another door, returning with towels and a robe. "This will help you get started. The bathroom," she said, pointing to a door on her left, "Is that way. Help yourself to a shower and any toiletries you need, and I'll look through my wardrobe and see what I can find that might fit you. You're a little curvier than me, but I should be able to wrangle something up."

Chynna's face split into a grin. "Thank you so much for the hospitality. I'm sorry to be a bother and take you away from whatever it was you were doing."

"No bother."

Minutes later, she was alone in the room. Chynna took the liberty of taking that much-needed shower in Rylee's fabulous mosaic-tiled shower. It didn't even have a door, so all she had to do was walk in, turn on the tap and let the rainfall showerhead pour over her. She used Rylee's almond-scented shampoo to wash her hair and her Carol's Daughter Almond Cookie body wash to scrub her skin. When she was all done, she rubbed the matching lotion all over her body.

She emerged from the shower to find Rylee had laid out some Levis and a print silk shirt and what looked like a new thong and a bra. *Where did she find new undergarments?* Chynna didn't ask. She just put them on and thankfully, they fit perfectly.

A knock sounded on the door. "Uh, c'mon," Chynna said, tentatively. It was Rylee's room after all.

The occupant of the room was on the other side. "Feel better?" Rylee walked over and touched the bruise on Chynna's forehead. She may just be a veterinarian, but she knew a contusion when she saw one.

"Hundred times," Chynna assured her, patting her hand away. "Thanks again and don't worry, this will heal."

"You're welcome," Rylee said. "So ..." She paused. "Do you want to tell me why you told my brother your name is Kenya?"

"Excuse me?"

Rylee grinned, revealing perfectly white teeth. "My brother may not listen to pop music, but I do. I know who you are, Chynna James."

Chynna blushed furiously. She'd hoped she wouldn't be recognized. That's what she got for thinking that just because they were on a ranch that they were hicks. "Sorry, I'm just trying to keep a low profile."

Rylee nodded. "I understand. The press has really been brutal about you and that actor Blake-what's-his-face."

"You have no idea, Rylee. It's been horrible, but I can assure you I'm no adulteress. I'm not having an affair with that man."

"Then why hide out and use your sister's name?"

"I'm tired of the constant scrutiny. They've been

hounding me for weeks, and I needed a break. No one can know I'm here."

"Chynna," Rylee sighed. "I don't keep secrets from my family."

"And I'm sorry to ask you to keep this one, but if the press finds out I'm here, it will be insanity for you and your family. Please, I'm asking you to keep my confidence."

Rylee stared at Chynna, clearly debating whether she should grant her request.

Chynna stared back at her with pleading eyes. If Rylee didn't agree, her and Kenya's plan would go up in smoke.

"Alright, as a guest in our home, you can trust me to keep your identity in the strictest of confidences."

Chynna came forward to grasp Rylee's hands and squeeze them. "Thank you. I appreciate that."

"You probably don't get that much."

Chynna released her hands and stepped backward. "You have no idea. Sometimes it's hard to know who to trust."

"You must have trusted Noah to get on the horse with a strange man and come to a strange place."

Chynna thought about Rylee's comment. She was right. She hadn't known Noah from a hole in the ground, but there was something about him. Was it his eyes or the way he carried himself that told her she could trust him? "Well, he'd already saved me from myself when I crashed into the fence. I figured he couldn't be half-bad."

Rylee laughed. "Those pesky cattle, how dare they get in the way?"

Chynna laughed along with her.

"Would you like that tour now? My parents will be materializing shortly for dinner."

Chynna glanced down at her watch and noticed it was nearly six p.m. *Where has the time gone?* It seemed only hours ago that she'd left the resort in search of the elusive hiking spot Kenya had mentioned. Speaking of which, Chynna wondered how her twin was doing. She hadn't heard from Kenya all day. How was she faring under the spotlight in her shoes?

6

"Alright, Chynna, let's go over the new routine one more time," the choreographer said as he coached Kenya through several intricate steps for a new dance routine to spice up the concert.

As soon as she and Lucas had landed, they'd been besieged by reporters eager to know where Chynna had been all this time and if she'd been on a rendezvous with Blake. She hadn't replied. Instead, Lucas scuttled her off into a limousine and they were driven to the studio for the tour rehearsal. Kenya hadn't so much as had a minute to prepare herself for what she was in for before she was thrown headfirst into the deep end.

Not only did she have to sing Chynna's music while learning a new dance in a skimpy pair of cutoff shorts and T-shirt that Penelope had laid out for her, but she had to do so with an audience of Deacon, Lucas, Fiona and Chynna's entire dance troupe. Kenya was beside herself with nerves, but she was trying hard not to show it.

"Are you alright, love?" the choreographer asked. "You're a little off today and usually you catch on to these things so quickly."

Kenya took Chynna's advice and didn't apologize. "Of course I'm alright. I've been doing this for five years, haven't I? Can't a girl have a bad day? Damn!"

The choreographer shrugged as if he was used to Chynna's theatrics, and he set about showing Kenya the steps again. She was going to be up all night practicing this routine to make sure she didn't make a fool out of herself on stage at Chynna's upcoming concert in Anaheim.

Kenya sauntered over to the director's chair next to Deacon and plopped herself down. "Deacon, would you be a dear and get me an Evian?"

"Sure, doll." He rose from his chair to do Kenya's bidding.

She couldn't believe he did it. She was perfectly capable of getting up to fetch her own water, but clearly that wasn't the way Chynna rolled. What she wasn't so happy about was Lucas staying at the studio to watch her. Why was he here? Chynna had indicated he'd never been interested in her romantically, so why stay on?

"Do you make a habit out of following all your acts?" Kenya asked Lucas as she accepted the towel her assistant handed her to wipe off sweat on her forehead.

"Only pop divas who make a habit of running off and refusing to tell their label where they're going," Lucas countered.

"Well, perhaps this *diva,*" Kenya said, turning around to give him a sideways glance, "needed a break from being managed. In case you hadn't noticed, I am capable of putting one foot in front of the other."

When Deacon approached her, Kenya rose, snatched the bottle of Evian he was offering and stormed back over to the choreographer to go over the steps again.

"What's up with her?" Lucas asked Deacon.

"I dunno," Deacon said, staring after her.

"She's pretty mouthy today."

"Isn't she always?"

"Not with me," Lucas stated, and he saw Deacon smile. "What?"

"You've given Chynna the cold shoulder for years," Deacon responded. "Perhaps she finally got the hint you're not interested."

Lucas didn't comment; instead, he continued to stare at Kenya, trying to figure out what it was that was different about her and why he was so intrigued.

An hour later, Kenya finished the session with the grand finale that she and the other dancers would complete at the end of the show. She'd gotten it down pat. *Whew, thank goodness!* She was getting worried that Chynna's entourage might begin to suspect she wasn't who she said she was, but so far, nothing.

"I'm ready to go home," Kenya said as she left the locker room after taking a long, hot shower. She'd dressed how she knew Chynna would, in a tank top, shorts, a short trench coat and her infamous shades.

"I'm afraid that's not on the agenda today," Deacon said. "You have a meeting with Carter Wright later."

"Today?" Kenya asked incredulously. She'd thought she'd have a little time for herself to call Chynna and see how she was enjoying her freedom.

"We've put the studio off long enough. They postponed rehearsals until you could come back. I think they were hoping that the furor over you and Blake would die down."

"No such luck," Kenya replied bitterly. The reporters waiting for them at the airport had been just as bad as Chynna had told her, probably worse since they'd had two weeks to wonder about her whereabouts.

"You knew you were going to have to face the music some time," Lucas replied from behind Kenya.

Sudden anger lit her eyes. She didn't need the two cents from the peanut gallery. "I know that. Just push back Carter for a few days, and I promise I'll see him soon."

"Alright," Deacon said. "I'll take care of it, but he won't be happy."

"In the meantime, I've put together a short press junket," Fiona jumped into the conversation. "You'll hit *Good Morning, America* and *Live with Kelly and Michael* before finishing up with Katie Couric."

"Are you kidding me?" Kenya asked. "Is all of this really necessary? It was just a stupid kiss for Christ's sake and not a very good one." She had hoped she and Chynna would switch back, and Chynna could clear her good name before Kenya would have to deal with all this nonsense.

Fiona looked horrified at Kenya's outburst. "You can't say that on national television. You have to be repentant and apologize for any miscommunication and that you never meant to hurt Blake's wife."

"That sounds an awful lot like admitting I did something wrong," Kenya replied. She couldn't believe the advice Chynna's team was giving her. *Why aren't they standing up for my sister and shouting from the rooftop that she isn't a slut?* "And I didn't do anything wrong. *He* kissed me. And *I* pushed him away."

Lucas watched Chynna from the side. He'd never seen her this vocal, this passionate about standing up for herself before. When it came to press matters, she usually did as Eli or Deacon and Fiona suggested.

Where had this combative, argumentative woman come from? He found it extremely sexy that she wasn't going to take this lying down. He understood it. Blake was married and the person at fault.

"I think Kenya's right," Lucas came to her defense. "I don't think she should be repentant. She should explain calmly and rationally that it was a miscommunication and that she's not interested in Blake."

"Then who?" Deacon asked. "Because you know the press isn't going to accept this lying down. We need to come out that she's been dating someone else for a while and not just anyone. Chynna James wouldn't date just anyone. We've got to make this good."

"Deacon's right," Fiona said. "We need someone young, hot, hip."

"Know any candidates?" Kenya asked Lucas flippantly. She watched one of his eyebrows rise at her direct question, but he didn't answer. Instead, he stared at her. His eyes never moved off hers in a battle of wills to see which of them would turn away first.

Kenya did. She couldn't take his intensity. It made her uncomfortable and not in a bad way. In made her hot in the nether regions.

"What about Emmett Griffin?" Fiona threw out.

"Isn't he dating that TV actress?" Deacon asked, pacing the floor as he tried to think of more eligible bachelors in Hollywood.

"How about Troy Raymond?"

"Not going to work," Deacon responded. "His sexual orientation has always been unclear. We can't have Chynna wrapped up in that mess."

"How about me?" Lucas offered.

"Say what?" Kenya's mouth hung open in disbelief.

"You need someone single," Lucas replied. "And I'm not seeing anyone at the moment."

"But, but th-that's ludicrous," Kenya stuttered and laughed nervously.

"No, it's ingenious," Deacon said, stopping in his tracks. "Everyone in your circle knows about your interest in Lucas."

Kenya colored in response because she could only imagine how embarrassing this conversation would be for Chynna, much less her. She couldn't think of anything worse than having to be next to Lucas for the next week, faking at being a couple to keep the press at bay. "Prior interest," she corrected, "which is why this won't work."

Lucas was shocked at Chynna's honesty. She'd just told him point-blank that she was no longer interested, and instead of feeling offended or hurt, he was even more excited.

"C'mon, Chynna, this is a great idea," Fiona piped up. "The paparazzi will think it's true and that you finally wore him down."

"What's wrong, Chynna?" Lucas eyed her suspiciously. "You would finally be getting what you wanted, if only for the cameras."

"I don't need a fake boyfriend," Kenya replied huffily, folding her arms across her chest. "I'm perfectly capable of obtaining one on my own."

"Oh, yeah?" Deacon asked. "So who do you have?"

Kenya's mouth pressed into a frown. She didn't have one of course. She just didn't want herself, or Chynna for that matter, to be railroaded into a fake romance with Lucas Kingston of all people. He rattled her and she wanted him far, far away.

"That's what I thought," Lucas replied. "I don't like this idea any better than you do, but I think it'll be salacious enough for the press to back off you and Blake."

"Are you prepared for the onslaught of the press that will be focused on you instead?" Fiona asked. "Because trust me, they'll be brutal."

"I didn't grow up in Beverly Hills, Fiona," Lucas returned. "I grew up on the streets of South Central. There's nothing the press can do to me I can't survive."

Kenya was impressed. She hadn't known much about Lucas's past, probably because Chynna didn't. But now she'd be forced into his company even more. And that spelled trouble. *What if he realizes I'm not really Chynna?*

"Then I'll set it up," Fiona said and rushed out of the room.

"Wait a second." Kenya held up her hand. "Don't I get say in this little charade?"

"No," Lucas stated emphatically. "It's been decided. You and I will stay close and the press hounds will be forced to move on from this notion that you're having an affair with a married man."

"Like hell!" Kenya stormed out of the room.

"I'll go talk to her." Deacon attempted to rise, but Lucas put a hand on his shoulder.

"Don't bother. I've got this," Lucas said and went in search of Chynna. Now this was the Chynna he remembered, behaving like a spoiled child when she didn't get her way. But he wasn't going to let her get in her own way and ruin her brand, a brand he and Eli had spent a lot of time developing.

He found Chynna pacing the hallway outside, and when he walked toward her, his initial intention had been to talk to her, to reason with her. But then she was standing there, full of piss and vinegar, and he'd gotten horny as hell. When he reached her, he grasped her by the shoulders, lowered his head and pressed his lips down on hers. He moved his mouth over hers, devouring its softness.

His actions must have shocked her because her hazel eyes widened with alarm and her hands went up to push him away, but he was stronger and wrapped his arms around her midriff, pulling her more firmly against him until they were thigh-to-thigh, chest-to-chest. He could feel her uneven breathing against his cheek. That's when he went in for the kill. His tongue teased at the seams of her lips until she surrendered and parted them to his invading tongue. She matched his passion and hunger, kiss for kiss, molding her body against him.

When he released her, Kenya stumbled back. The kiss Lucas had just given her sent a lightning bolt right up her spine, and she was slightly dizzy. Her heart hammered at what had just happened between them.

Lucas's silence told Kenya that he'd felt it too. Something inextricable that couldn't be explained. "I ... I'm sorry," Lucas began, and then must have thought better of it because he changed tactics and said, "Actually, no, I'm not. The press is going to be all over us and we need to make this relationship believable."

Kenya breathed in deeply, forcing air into her lungs to calm her steady heartbeat. *So that mind-blowing kiss was him acting?* She would be afraid to see how he would kiss if he wasn't.

When she'd sufficiently recovered, she said, "I never said I was going to participate in this farce."

"Chynna." He sounded exasperated. "You must see that giving the press something new will get them off this news cycle of you and Blake. Don't you want that? Or do you like being an infamous homewrecker."

Kenya's fair cheeks burned with fury. "Of course not. I want to clear my name."

"Well then, get on board," Lucas said, and seconds later he'd spun on his heel and hall leaving a stunned Kenya in his absence.

Once away from the beguiling diva, Lucas could think clearly. *What has gotten into me, offering myself as bait to lure the press off Chynna's supposed affair?* He'd always been in the background of R&K Records, letting Eli work the press angle and here he was purposely putting himself out there. The press would be relentless; wanting to know intimate details about his and Chynna's supposed relationship. *And why did I do it?* Because in a mere twenty-four hours, Chynna James had suddenly become more to him that just an artist; she'd become a full-fledged, sexy woman with a backbone, and she was damn hard to ignore. *But now what?*

AFTER EVERYONE, including Deacon and Fiona, had mercifully left Kenya alone, save her bodyguards posted outside, she finally made her way into the Chynna's room mansion. Every move she made, everywhere she'd gone today, someone was there. *How does Chynna take the incessant people flittering around her all day?*

Kenya was exhausted as she walked up the marble staircase she would call home for the next week. Chynna's master bedroom, if that's what you would call it, was unlike anything Kenya had in her small one-bedroom apartment in New York. Her place wasn't grand—it was regal. The four-poster canopy bed with draped silks in Chynna's room was nothing short of breathtaking.

She couldn't resist throwing herself on the bed and allowing her fingers to roam over the luxurious fabrics and sumptuous pillows. This was how the other one and a half percent lived. *I could get used to this.* But then, her mind went to that kiss with Lucas. *Where did all the heat come from?*

She'd thought Chynna told her Lucas had never shown interest in her, but tonight, he'd shown that he was not as immune to Chynna as she'd once thought or perhaps *she* was the difference? *Is Lucas seeing something in me that he has never seen in Chynna?* She had responded to him with complete and utter abandon, as if she weren't imitating her sister. She couldn't let it happen again or she was headed for disaster.

Kenya sighed and closed her eyes. When she reopened them, she saw Chynna's closet. Kenya rushed over and swung open the double doors. She was greeted with a large walk-in closet fit for a queen. She walked inside, admiring the rows and rows of clothes, shoes, and purses. The middle cabinet held scarves, belts and other accessories. And all of this was hers for two weeks! Kenya could hardly believe it.

She grabbed a Dolce & Gabbana outfit off the hanger to try and then Marc Jacobs, and Michael Kors, and before she knew it, she'd stuffed loads of clothes under her arms. She stripped to her skivvies so she could try them all on. Her reflection in the mirror with each new outfit told her that she looked darn good in expensive clothes. And combined with the shoes, well, combined they probably cost more than her flat in New York.

Kenya turned sideways to stare again at herself. Of course, this would all come to an end soon, but that didn't mean she couldn't enjoy it. Perhaps it wasn't so bad living in Chynna's shoes after all.

7

The tour of the Hart estate took nearly half an hour because Rylee had to show Chynna the fitness, game and movie rooms, business offices, racquet court, indoor pool with Jacuzzi, sauna and massage room. It was very impressive, even to Chynna, because it made her ten-bedroom mansion in Beverly Hills look like a child's place. She'd bought the house four years ago, but rarely had the time to enjoy it. When she wasn't on tour for nine months out of the year, she was in the studio recording or in the gym or practicing a dance routine. But the Hart estate was really a home because they actually used the rooms instead of having them for show.

"My parents should be in the living room," Rylee said as she led Chynna there. And she was correct. Isaac and Madelyn Hart were sitting on a plush sofa. He was holding a tumbler of scotch, and his beautiful wife was holding a glass with red wine.

Isaac Hart was an honest-looking man. He had a slightly receding salt-and-pepper hairline, a round face with a broad nose like Noah's and big dimpled cheeks. Even though he was seated, Chynna could see where Noah got his stature and broad, but basketball-player-build, because he was his father's spitting image. Isaac was wearing a blazer, plaid shirt, pressed jeans and pristine-looking cowboy boots, but his impressive physique had clearly withstood the test of time.

Noah was also present and was standing next to the mantel dressed similarly in a plaid shirt and jeans, except his seemed more snug-fitting and hugged his ample behind. Noah was just as sexy and handsome as when Chynna had awoken from her crash to see his dark-brown eyes staring down at hers with concern, except this time, when he laid eyes on Chynna and Rylee, his expression turned surly. What could she have possibly done just by walking in the room to change his disposition?

He quickly averted his gaze from Chynna and flashed it toward his sister. "Did you give Kenya here the two-cent tour?"

"Of course." Rylee smiled genuinely. "She is a guest in our home."

"Kenya, welcome." Madelyn Hart rose from the sofa to greet her.

Chynna started to speak up, but once Madelyn Hart reached her, she tugged one of her arms into the crook of Chynna's and led her to a nearby loveseat. "Noah told us that you had a quite a fright today when your Jeep hit our fence. Are you alright, my dear?" She seemed genuinely concerned for Chynna's safety. "Should we contact a doctor to check you out?"

"That's really not necessary," Chynna said as she sat down next to Madelyn. "I'm okay, really. Rylee checked me out."

"Yeah, she was playing the tough chick from the start," Noah replied laughingly. "Said the cows made her do it."

"Noah!" his mother admonished. "That's not very nice of you to make fun. Kenya here could have been hurt."

"I did the gentlemanly thing, didn't I?" he asked, glancing in Chynna's direction. "I checked her out for a concussion and brought her back here."

"Reluctantly, I might add," Chynna said underneath her breath. Rylee was standing near her and heard her comment. "Yes, you did," she added. "And I'm very grateful for your hospitality, Mrs. Hart." There was something about Madelyn that made Chynna feel warm and fuzzy. She reminded her of what it could be like if her mother was still around.

Madelyn Hart was the opposite of her mother, though. Madelyn Hart had a big personality. She commanded authority, not by her loud voice but by her regal presence. Her stylishly cut salt-and-pepper bob hung in curls around her face, and she wore a crisp, white wraparound top, cinched at the side, and a pair of fitted black capris. Chynna could tell the cowboy boots she wore were expensive and made of the finest leather or perhaps alligator?

And it was clear everyone in Madelyn's family, from her children to her husband, adored her. When she'd walked into the living room, the Harts had been holding hands and whispering to each other. Chynna had never seen a genuinely happily married couple before. Her parents had divorced when she and Kenya were so young that she barely remembered when her parents had been together.

"You're most welcome." Madelyn patted her thigh and then she turned back to her eldest son. "Any idea where your wayward brother, Caleb, is? It's dinnertime, and you know how I feel about eating together as a family."

"Dunno." Noah shrugged. "Probably at one of his rodeo events."

"I told that boy to stay away from those rodeos," Isaac huffed. "He could get hurt if one of those bulls get a hold of 'em."

"You know Caleb, Dad," Noah replied. "He loves living life on the edge."

"Will get him killed one day," his father responded.

"I sure hope not," Madelyn said. "My youngest," she said, turning to Chynna, "has always been somewhat of a daredevil."

"You mean reckless," Noah countered.

"Well, everyone can't be you—the perfect son," Rylee commented. "Some of us make mistakes." She'd sure made her share of mistakes, most recently by dating Jeremy, her parent's choice of a spouse for her. She and Jeremy couldn't have less in common. The only thing she was sure of was being the best veterinarian possible and making a name for herself, which hadn't been so easy. She'd disobeyed her father by choosing to go to college. He'd expected her to be the dutiful daughter, to be a ranch wife and make some babies. He'd been sorely disappointed when she'd opted for another life instead. But Rylee wouldn't change her decision for anything in the world.

"That's right. Go ahead and make excuses for him, Rylee," Noah replied, "like you've always done. Let's forget that he should be here at the ranch helping the family."

"Now, now," Madelyn jumped in. "Let's not get riled up before dinner. We have a guest with us tonight."

Chynna didn't mind the squabbling between the

siblings; it showed they were a family who truly cared about each other. She envied their closeness.

Madelyn rose from the sofa. "Well, if Caleb isn't going to join us, how about some diner?"

"Sounds good to me." Her husband stood up, and soon they all followed suit and joined the elder Harts, who were heading for the dining room.

NOAH SAT UNEASILY next to their houseguest at the dinner table. Rylee had circumvented him by sitting across from Kenya, leaving him no choice but to sit next to her while his parents sat at either head of the table. Sitting this close, Noah could smell her. He didn't know what fragrance she had on, but smoky and spicy suited her. It was nothing like the sweet, rosy scents Maya used to wear.

Perhaps that's what bothered him the most about this stranger. She oozed sexuality from every pore, even though she was dressed simply in a pair of Rylee's old jeans and a silk shirt with a few buttons casually opened at the neck, just enough for Noah to see the slight swell of her breasts. Maya, God rest her soul, was classically beautiful, and although Noah found her breathtaking, he'd never had such a primal response to her physicality before. Kenya's hair had been kissed by the sun. Her skin held a golden hue that shined. She probably was of mixed heritage somewhere down the line.

"Noah, did you hear me?" his mother asked.

Noah blinked to clear the fog that was Kenya from his brain. "What was that, Mama?"

"I asked how the thirty-fifth anniversary celebrations were coming along."

"Very good, ma'am," Noah replied. "We're booked

for this weekend. We have the mayor and several councilmen coming to the last night of the event."

"Did you say thirty-fifth anniversary?" Chynna asked. Her voice rose slightly, and she glanced at Rylee but tried hard not to show her alarm.

"Yes," Madelyn answered. "Isaac and I have owned this ranch for over thirty-five years. We made a go of it as a ranch for the first twenty years, but once I started having the kids, it was just too difficult to keep it going solely as a working ranch."

"That's when they turned it into a dude ranch," Noah picked up, "and opened it up to the public to stay on the ranch and have a true Western experience."

"Congratulations," Chynna said. "It's amazing the success you've had in just a decade." She'd thought they'd been doing this for far longer than that, because the ranch was so well-manicured.

"It wasn't always this easy," Isaac said. "We started out with five cabins and only a few guests to help supplement our income, but eventually we expanded thanks to Noah's expertise here."

Chynna glanced sideways at Noah. "Is that so?"

"I'm not just some dumb cowboy," Noah replied, "though most people might think that."

"I don't." Chynna was horrified he'd think otherwise.

"I have a master's degree in Business Administration. And once I received my diploma, I came back to the ranch to help Mom and Dad expand. Now we have fifty cabins on the estate."

Chynna offered a smile. "That's impressive."

"So what is it you do?" Noah inquired. He was curious about Kenya and why she'd come to Canyon

Ranch to escape the real world like the other socialites.

She paused as if unsure of what to say, and Noah wondered if she was trying to come up with a good lie, but eventually she said, "I'm an actress."

"An actress?" His interest was piqued. "What have you done? Would I know something?"

"Noah, give the woman a chance to speak," Rylee said, jumping in as if the questions he was asking were unreasonable.

Chynna reached for her water glass, and he saw her hand tremble as she nervously sat it back down on the table. "A small show on TV."

"I don't have much time on my hands with taking care of the ranch to watch much television," Noah replied.

"Did you always know you wanted to be an actress?" Madelyn asked, changing to a more general question.

Chynna nodded. "I have. In school, I was always singing or acting in some play, and eventually, I landed some roles on Broadway."

"Sounds like an exciting life," Noah replied, taking a sip of wine. "So why were you at Canyon Ranch—trying to get away from it?"

Chynna turned and gave him a hostile glare. "Not getting away really, just a vacation."

Noah nodded, but he didn't really believe her. She seemed to be hiding something, but he couldn't put his finger on what that was. He was curious to find out what secret a woman like her could possibly have. She seemed to have it all, yet she seemed unhappy with her life. Noah wondered if he'd find out why.

. . .

THE NEXT MORNING, Chynna rose early to watch the sunrise. Thanks to Kenya, she was getting used to the early morning, watching the day start and getting in a run. At first, she'd been resistant to getting up, but eventually, Kenya had convinced her, and now, Chynna was starting to enjoy getting a good start to the day.

She looked through Rylee's enormous wardrobe and found a simple white tank top and running shorts she could wear. Pulling on her tennis shoes, she went to explore the Golden Oaks Ranch.

At six a.m., the house was quiet save for the wind chimes blowing in the breeze. Chynna made her way outside just as sunlight began streaming through the clouds.

"C'mon, boy," she heard a masculine voice mutter.

Chynna followed the sound of the voice out to the bullpen by the barn and saw Noah shirtless and wrangling with the stallion he'd been riding when he'd first rescued her.

The sight of Noah with sweat glistening off his hairless chest took Chynna by surprise. He was so magnificently rugged and manly she had to force air into her lungs as a rush of lust surged through her. Her heart jolted, and her pulse began to pound.

As if sensing he was not alone, Noah turned around to find her staring at him from the corner. "Do you always sneak up on people ... wearing next to nothing?" he asked, taking her in from head to toe. His eyes didn't miss a beat as he perused her skimpy tank top and shorts. Rylee was much more slender than Chynna, so her shorts didn't cover much.

"Not usually," Chynna replied to Noah's question. She found her voice despite the tightening she felt in her breasts when he stared at her like that. His eyes seemed to zero in on them for the merest of seconds before returning back to his horse and task. "And I have on clothes."

"Very little," he mumbled.

"Do you always get up this early?" Chynna asked, lifting one leg and then the other over the fence so she could jump inside the bullpen with him.

The Arabian horse became skittish as Chynna approached and began pacing around the pen away from Noah.

"What do you think you're doing?" he asked, glancing at her.

"I just wanted to see what you're doing."

"Well, Max doesn't like visitors."

"Kind of like you?" Chynna said, raising an eyebrow. He hadn't disguised the fact he was less than pleased to have her as a house-guest.

Noah looked disconcerted for a minute. Had she finally caught him off-kilter?

"What do you mean?"

"I know you don't think of much of socialites who go to Canyon Ranch, and apparently, actresses fall into that category as well."

Noah laughed. It was the first time Chynna had heard him laugh. It was rich and throaty, and he needed to do it more often because when he did, his whole face softened and he was instantly more approachable.

"Ms. James." Noah walked toward her. "I don't have an opinion of you one way or the other."

Chynna sauntered toward him, her hips swaying in each direction. "I disagree. I believe you said socialites wouldn't be caught dead here on your ranch."

"I did because it's true. They or you for that matter wouldn't last a week on my ranch." Noah turned his back to her and began speaking softly to the Arabian horse.

Chynna's eyes narrowed. She hated when someone told her she couldn't do something. When folks back home thought she wouldn't be a successful singer, she'd proved them wrong and look where she was now—one of the biggest stars of the millennium. "Then I'll prove you wrong."

"What did you say?" He turned around with a confused expression.

"I'm going to stay at this ranch for a week and prove to you that this actress and socialite can do more than just get mani-pedis and do yoga."

Noah stopped brushing the horse and let the brush fall to the ground. He walked toward her with a fierce purpose. "You don't have anything to prove to me, Kenya."

Chynna stood upright and stuck out her chest. "I know that." She didn't have anything to prove to him, but maybe she had something to prove to herself—that she was more than just a pretty face, that she actually had some grit to take her life back in her own hands.

Noah leaned back and stared at her long and hard before saying, "I'm calling your bluff, Kenya James. Go change out of those skimpy clothes and put on some real cowgirl clothes, and I'll put you through the paces."

An easy smile reached Chynna's mouth. Noah was actually taking her seriously. She didn't know what she was getting herself into, but she had a feeling that the next week was about to change her life.

. . .

"ARE you sure you want to do this?" Rylee asked Chynna as she took her through the general store at the ranch later that morning so Chynna could buy some clothes rather than wear Rylee's hand-me-downs.

Chynna spun around on her heel at the doubt in Rylee's voice. "You don't think I can do this?"

"It's not that—"

"Sounds like it," Chynna replied.

"Have you ever been on a horse?"

"I've been horseback riding several times."

"Horseback riding a few times and helping Noah during roundup is a completely different scenario," Rylee said.

"Why does everyone think they know what's best for me?" asked Chynna. "It's so frustrating not to be taken seriously."

Rylee touched Chynna's shoulder, and she jumped away. "Is that why you needed a break from your real life?"

Chynna rolled her eyes upward. "You have no idea, Rylee. My label, my manager, my publicist, they all think I'm an idiot who has to be led around by the nose. I'm not a horse that just does their bidding. I have my own thoughts and ideas."

"Then you need to stand up for yourself."

"I know." Tears formed in Chynna's eyes. "And I will. I'm taking my life into my own hands, starting now. I have to do this, Rylee. Not just to show Noah I'm not an airhead, but to prove to myself that I'm capable of more—to find that strong Chynna I know exists."

"Then you have my support," Rylee said. "I have your back."

"Thank you, because I think I'm going to need it."

. . .

AFTER SHE'D FOUND some clothes at the general store and changed into a pair of jeans and a plaid shirt, Chynna headed to the stables to find Noah. She had no idea just how hard *or how smelly* manual labor was until Noah had her cleaning out the horses' stalls and adding fresh hay. She doubted she would ever forget the smell of manure.

"Ready for a break?" Noah asked, poking his head into the last stall Chynna was working on.

"Just about," Chynna said, wiping the sweat from her forehead with a bandana she'd bought at the store.

Noah smiled broadly. He seemed surprised that after four hours she hadn't given up and begged to be taken back to Canyon Ranch for a manicure and pedicure.

"Lunch is ready," he said. "C'mon. I'll buy you a glass of ice cold lemonade."

She didn't need to be asked twice. Chynna quickly threw the dreaded rack down on the stall floor and followed Noah outside. Thank God she'd had the good sense to buy a cowboy hat and some sunglasses, because the sky was clear and the sun was shining brightly when they emerged from the stables.

Chynna noticed that they were not heading to the main house, but rather were going toward the Golden Oaks Ranch café. "We're not going to the house?"

Noah glanced back at her. "You said you wanted to be treated like everyone else. Well, they don't get an invite to the main house for lunch. They eat here in the corral with the guests."

Chynna held her tongue from making a scorching comeback and said, "Of course." She followed him into the air-conditioned café that was full to capacity with the day's lunch crowd, everyone from paid guests to ranch hands. Before she could wonder where they were going to sit, a tall, dark-skinned man yelled Noah's name across the room, and they headed toward his table in the corner.

Noah turned to Chynna at his side. "Jonas, this is Kenya. She's a guest of the family but wants to experience the ranch like a true cowgirl."

She knew he didn't believe she could do it, and she gave a twisted smile as Noah held out her chair. *Ever the gentleman,* she thought.

When the waitress brought over a pitcher of lemonade without asking, Chynna wasted no time leaning over to grab it and pour herself a generous glass. She leaned back and chugged the cool drink. When she looked up, both men were staring at her.

"Thirsty?" Noah's brown eyes were laughing.

"As a matter of fact, I was." She looked over to Jonas. "Your boss is quite the slave driver. He put me out there in the hot stables and didn't even leave me with water. I bet he does more for his horses."

Jonas turned to Noah and gave him a surprised look. Noah merely shrugged.

"So, how long are you staying, Miss Kenya?" Jonas asked.

"Dunno, a week, maybe two."

"Two weeks?" Noah sputtered the lemonade he'd been drinking. He'd known she said a week, but he wasn't sure he could take that many cold showers. Just being near Kenya had raised his libido.

Clearly, he'd thought she wouldn't be around very long. Was his treatment of her today a way to keep her at arm's length and make her leave sooner?

The waitress reappeared to take their order.

Chynna was so hungry after her strenuous morning that she ordered the pulled- pork sandwich and French fries. If she was in L.A., she wouldn't dream of having the carbs and fried food, but she was living like a Tucson local.

Lunch with Noah and Jonas was more fun than Chynna expected. Noah was relaxed around the other man and, in turn, was much better company, cracking jokes and telling stories that made Chynna's stomach hurt from laughing so hard. When was the last time she'd truly laughed because she was having fun? *Too long.*

"Kenya?"

She glanced up and realized Noah had been speaking to her. "Yes?"

"I asked if you were ready to get back to work."

"Sure." She rose to her feet, and Noah was right there to pull out her chair. "Thanks," she said as she passed him by.

NOAH INHALED DEEPLY as Kenya breezed past him and caught that feminine scent that was uniquely hers. When she was around, he felt different and more aware of a female than he'd ever been since Maya passed. And he didn't like it. It made him feel guilty because Kenya had him thinking lustful thoughts of taking her to bed and how she would sound when he made her come.

Reluctantly, he shook Jonas's hand and followed her out the door. She was waiting for him outside.

"What's next?"

"Not ready to throw in the towel yet?"

She raised an eyebrow. "No, plus I doubt you've even gotten started."

He laughed. He hadn't. He was taking it easy on her for now, but if she continued to keep up this charade for a week, let alone two, it would drive him mad with lust. And he would be forced to play hardball to keep her at bay. "C'mon," he said, and instead of going back to the stables, he took her to the petting farm.

Several families and their small children were congregating throughout the farm area, petting animals ranging from rabbits to sheep to goats to llamas. Kenya didn't strike him as the type who loved children or animals, so this would be excellent payback.

She looked up at him warily, and Noah knew he'd hit the nail on the head. Kenya had never been around animals other than horses. "What do I have to do?"

"Why don't you help Nancy here with the kids and animals," Noah said, coming toward an older Caucasian woman with leathery skin from the sun. She wore jeans and a similar plaid shirt like Kenya's, except her colorful cowboy boots were worn and decorated with horseshoes and arrows.

"How so?"

Noah didn't answer her; he merely continued walking toward Nancy.

"Mr. Noah," Nancy said, nodding to him. "What can I do you for?"

"My guest here, Kenya, is living like a ranch hand for the week. I thought she could help you here in the petting farm, like filling up the feeds, helping with the children ..." His voice trailed off.

"Sure thing, Mr. Noah." Nancy smiled warmly as he turned to leave. "C'mon, Kenya, I'll get you started."

Kenya held up a finger. "Wait a second." She caught up with Noah at the entrance to the farm and lightly touched his arm.

The tiny gesture didn't escape him, and he met her

light- brown eyes with his own dark-brown ones. They stared at each other for what seemed like an eternity, and he wasn't imagining the heat emanating between them. When she eventually removed her hand, his arm felt as if she'd singed him.

Kenya nervously shifted from one foot to the other. "Listen, I ... I don't know anything about animals, let alone children." He watched her glance down at a small boy who couldn't have been more than five years old who'd followed her to the entrance.

Noah couldn't help smiling as he knew this was far out of her league. "You'll be fine. Nancy will take good care of you. I'll see you back at the main house for dinner. Six o'clock sharp. Mom hates when we're late."

He quickly turned on his heel and fled from the farm as quickly as he could, because if he didn't, he'd take the beguiling actress in his arms and kiss her until they were both senseless.

8

"Do you have time to go over the facts on Lucas in the dossier I e-mailed you this morning?" Fiona asked Kenya over lunch on the deck of Chynna's estate.

"I already did." Kenya gulped some of the strawberry fruit smoothie she'd just inhaled after a grueling two-hour workout session with Chynna's trainer.

Fiona gave her a disbelieving look, but Kenya didn't care. She was exhausted and the day had only just begun. Her intent had been to sleep in after a late night until she was due back at the dance studio to rehearse for the tour. She had no idea Chynna's beefed-up trainer with Hercules-sized arms would wake her and ask her to do a warrior workout at six a.m.

She hadn't known what a warrior workout entailed, but she'd soon found out. The trainer, named Doug, had Kenya running six laps around the estate, doing a hundred lunges, a hundred push-ups and a hundred sit-ups before embarking on jumping rope, pushing tires and performing burpees in her home fitness center until she lost count. Kenya thought she'd been in shape with running three miles a day, but nothing had prepared her for Doug. He pushed her so hard that by the end of the workout, her T-shirt was soaking wet.

Kenya had happily bid him *adieu* at eight a.m., so she could mercifully sit at her kitchen counter and watch her personal chef create a strawberry and banana smoothie. It may have been Chynna's favorite, but Kenya despised bananas and it took every effort in her being to finish half the smoothie.

"Alright, if you looked this over, tell me where he grew up?" Fiona inquired.

"South Central."

"What college did he attend?"

"UCLA."

Fiona eyed her suspiciously and looked down at her fact sheet. "And how did he get the money to start R&K Records?"

"He convinced several of his college buddies to loan him the money before buying them out."

Fiona looked up in surprise. "You really did study this, didn't you?"

"You sound surprised," Kenya said, watching Fiona carefully. She had to be sure she wasn't overplaying her hand.

"Well ... it does usually take you a few times to remember interview answers."

"Well ...," Kenya mimicked her, "I need to be prepared. If I'm going to go on all the talk shows and convince them Lucas and I are legit, I need to know him like the back of my hand, correct?"

"Of course, of course," Fiona replied. "I didn't mean otherwise. It's just so unlike you to be so—"

"Prepared?" Kenya finished.

Fiona shrugged and didn't answer.

"What else do you have for me today?" Kenya replied testily. She had to remember that Chynna wouldn't stand for this kind of doubt from her employees.

Before Fiona could answer, Penelope came and placed several photographs in front of Kenya. "I need you to sign these promotion shots, please."

Kenya scribbled her signature across the first document, realized her mistake and ripped the photo into pieces.

"What's wrong?" Penelope asked.

"Nothing," Kenya snapped, reminding herself that Chynna didn't have to answer anyone. "I asked what's on my agenda for today. Can one of you ..." She paused, looking at Fiona and Penelope, then picked up another photo to sign, "help me out here? I don't have all day." Kenya knew she sounded like a bitch and hated behaving this way, but she was Chynna after all and her sister was known for her sometimes bad behavior.

"We have to go shopping for a dress for you for Lucas's party tomorrow," Penelope said.

"And you have to make an appearance," Fiona threw in. "And I've come up with a memorable one."

"Oh, yeah?" Kenya acted as if she was bored signing the photographs and looked up from the task. "What's the idea?"

"You're going to pop out of Lucas's birthday cake, à la Marilyn Monroe and sing 'Happy Birthday.'"

Kenya let out an exaggerated sigh. "Fiona, you've got to be kidding me."

"I think it's a great idea," Fiona huffed. "Just the sort of thing the public will expect from you, something over the top to express your love and adoration for your new man."

"It just seems so cliché."

Penelope chuckled. "Maybe, but it's exactly something you would do."

"Fine!" Kenya threw her hands up in defeat. She had to remember that *she* wasn't the one who would be jumping out of the cake, but rather Chynna. Her sister's image was of a fun, single party girl, but it was also the image she was trying to avoid, maybe even fix for her twinie.

"We have to find a super-sexy outfit for the occasion," Penelope said, even though she dressed the exact opposite. "One that will show off your figure and have men, including Lucas, drooling."

Kenya rolled her eyes upward. The sexifying of her sister was something that was perpetrated by her record label and apparently amped up by her entire team. *Has everyone forgotten that Chynna is a normal human being underneath this sex kitten image they've created?*

"Great, what else?"

"Then you have your dance rehearsal and a meeting with Carter."

Kenya rubbed her hands in glee. Now this she was looking forward to. To meet a great director like Carter Wright was the icing on the cake of imitating her sister.

Two hours later at an exclusive boutique on Rodeo Drive, Kenya had tried on several form-fitting dresses that fit like a second skin on her behind, but eventually she, Penelope, and Fiona had settled on one: a reverse V-neck, cutout mini-dress that would shock, awe and inspire envious glances. This cocktail dress had a sexy piping, corset-style top with V-neckline and exquisite lace trim with a padded bust that made her breasts look like they were tumbling out. Megan was styling the dress with dangling spike earrings, finished with high-gloss stilettos and a sequined clutch.

"You are rocking that dress," Fiona said from the sidelines. "And when Lucas sees you in it, he's going to wish he was dating you for real."

"Thanks." Kenya gave a half-hearted smile. "I'm going to get undressed and ready for dance rehearsal." As she closed the door behind her to the dressing room, that very same scenario was what Kenya was afraid of. That kiss from Lucas the other night was a complication she hadn't expected and certainly didn't need. She didn't need Lucas trying to get close to her, *to Chynna* this week. She needed to keep him at bay because if he should get too close, he might realize the truth. If that should happen, it was only a matter of time before Chynna would have to come forward, and Kenya didn't want that. Not just because Chynna needed the time and space away from the spotlight, but because as hard as it was, it was kind of fun to be someone else for a change. Kenya was enjoying stepping outside herself for a while and trying something new.

LUCAS STARED at the latest sales reports for his low-performing artists, but it might as well have been in a foreign language because he couldn't focus on them. He threw them down on his cherry wood desk and leaned back in his executive chair and rubbed his head.

Chynna. Damn that woman. She'd been in his thoughts ever since that kiss last night. Rather than review sales, he'd much prefer to be at the dance rehearsal watching Chynna sashay those curves of hers across the dance floor, watch the sweat form on her bosom and wish that she was sweating underneath him as he pumped deep inside her.

Oh Lord!! Lucas shook his head. What the hell was happening to him? He'd never been this horny for a woman before and certainly not without acting on it to relieve himself. Problem was, the moment he'd decided he'd like to take Chynna James to bed was the moment she'd decided she was no longer interested. Of course, her response to him last night had proved she wasn't as immune to him as she protested, yet that brought him little solace. He was not used to having to court to get a woman's favor. With his stature in Hollywood, women came to him. So, it was a bit disconcerting that he might actually have to romance a woman.

Lucas chuckled. *Guess I'm about to find out if chivalry isn't dead after all.*

KENYA WAS nervous yet excited as she sat waiting for Carter Wright to come into his office. Several minutes ago, his perky brunette assistant had let her in and offered her a bottle of Perrier, but Kenya was too nervous to drink. She'd dreamed of working with Carter her entire career, but the odds of an unknown actress such as herself on an underrated television series getting that opportunity was slim to none; but here she was in his office.

She knew she wasn't there based on her own talents, but rather Chynna's name, but that still didn't mean she wouldn't give the performance of her life and convince him that Chynna was worth keeping on the film and not replacing with another actress. She'd done her homework and read the script from cover to cover.

Kenya was so deep in her thoughts that she didn't hear Carter come into the room until he was standing right in front of her.

"Well, if it isn't the elusive Chynna James," Carter said. He glanced around the room. "And without her entourage," he said with a thin-lipped smile. "I'm impressed."

Kenya rose from her chair with self-assured confidence to face the older Caucasian gentlemen. He was a tall man with nearly white hair and a beer belly, but he was a master of film. "I'm perfectly capable of speaking with you myself."

Carter raised an eyebrow. "Someone's feeling confident today. Perhaps your two-week stint in obscurity played a part?"

Kenya walked toward him and stared him directly in the eye. "I took some much needed time off, not only to allow the vultures time to cool their heels, but also to get my head back on straight and prepare myself for this film."

"I'm not sure there will be a film," Carter responded. "The producers are skittish about pairing you and Blake together again after this incident. Blake and Giselle are America's sweethearts, and you're viewed as the interloper. They think the movie will tank if we move forward, and I can't say that I disagree with them, especially given your performance prior to this debacle."

Shit. Shit. Shit. Chynna didn't need this. Kenya needed to salvage Chynna's film career. She couldn't let it go up in smoke before it had even gotten started. "I appreciate your candor, Carter," Kenya replied, "but I can assure you my performance will be much improved."

"You couldn't deliver your lines with one shred of emotion."

"Try me," Kenya boasted. She knew she was a damn good actress and could convince Carter Wright of Chynna's capabilities.

"Alright, Chynna, you're on." He went behind his desk and pressed the intercom button. "Suzie, get me Liam for a reading."

"Yes, Mr. Wright," said the female voice on the other end.

Kenya pulled off the cropped leather jacket that Megan had paired with her edgy skintight leather leggings and poplin white shirt, and she prepared to knock the socks off the director. He expected Chynna would be nervous and unprepared, but Kenya was going to deliver a stellar performance.

Several minutes later, a ruddy-faced, blond man came into the office. "You wanted to see, Mr. Wright?"

Carter waved him inside. "I sure did. I want you to read with Ms. James." He flipped open the script. "Scene twelve."

Kenya knew the scene intimately. It was a scene that required Chynna to give a nuanced performance of sadness at losing her daughter before giving way to passion between her and the hero, which in this case, would be Liam. Carter was sure hitting below the belt with this one. Kenya wasn't sure Chynna would have been able to pull off the scene in a cold read, but Kenya was a seasoned pro. She was used to working with actors she didn't know.

She sat down on the sofa and put her head in her hands. "I can't believe she's gone," Kenya wailed. "She's all that I had."

"I'm sorry, Yvette," Liam said, reading his lines. "This must be difficult for you."

Kenya shook her head in despair. "I, I had no idea she was suffering. To, to find out this way ... at the end, when there's no hope of recovery." Kenya jumped off from the sofa and paced the room. "It's not fair. How could this happen? How could I not know that my own child was sick?"

"You mustn't blame yourself."

"It's hard not to. I'm the parent, and I could lose my baby girl." Kenya glanced up at him with tears in her eyes. "What am I going to do?"

Liam placed the script down and came toward Kenya. "I don't know, sweetheart, but I'm here for you." He lifted her cheek with one hand, and Kenya looked into his blue eyes. "If you ever need me for anything, I'm here."

Kenya let the seconds pass before she reached up and circled her hands around Liam's neck. "I need you now," she whispered. Seconds later, she kissed him with such passion that it took him by surprise, but not for long because he actually kissed her back.

"Cut!" Carter yelled from behind his desk.

Kenya pulled away from Liam, who looked like he had stars in his eyes from kissing *the* Chynna James, and she turned to the director. "So, how did I do?"

Ten minutes later, Kenya walked out of Carter's office on top of the world. She'd convinced the surly director that Chynna had what it took for the role and that she was focused on the task at hand. She'd told him the notoriety would only lend itself to the film because people would want to go see if the rumors were true. Carter wasn't sure he could convince the producers, but he was going to give it the old college try.

When she slid into the limo waiting for her outside of the studio offices, Deacon was waiting for her inside. "Well?" he asked anxiously, ending the call he'd been on. "How did it go?"

Kenya smiled, revealing even, white teeth. Deacon hadn't been pleased when she'd insisted on going into the meeting with Wright by herself. He'd said she'd never met with him previously on her own, but Kenya had convinced Deacon that she needed to show Carter that she could stand on her own two feet. And she'd done exactly that.

"How do you think it went?" she said snarkily, getting back into character. "I knocked his socks off."

"Good girl." Deacon patted her thigh. "I always knew you could do this. I don't know why you've been so down on yourself about your acting capability."

"I just needed some time away."

"The time with your sister clearly did the trick," Deacon said. "I'm going to have to remember to utilize her more often."

Kenya turned sharply to glare at Deacon. "My sister is not someone you can use to whip me into shape."

Deacon lowered his head at Kenya's crisp tone. "I'm sorry. That wasn't how I meant it."

"How did you mean it?"

"Only that if I'd known Kenya was your happy place, I would make sure your schedule permitted you to see her more often."

"Oh, okay," Kenya said, leaning back into the plush limo cushions. She wanted to be sure Chynna's entourage didn't view her as a weapon they could use at will.

"I'm on your side, kiddo," Deacon said, slapping her knee. "Always have been."

Kenya offered a weak smile. "I know." She didn't know, but she hoped Chynna could depend on him.

. . .

"BIGGER, SHE NEEDS BIGGER HAIR," Fiona told Derrick who was completing Kenya's look for Lucas's birthday party the following evening. She was going to have to jump out of the birthday cake in the lacy bustier dress they'd found earlier in the day and sing "Happy Birthday" to Lucas. A few strategically placed members of the legitimate press and paparazzi would be on hand for the event. Fiona was sure the theatrical entrance would set their tongues wagging and have the press wondering what was going on between Lucas Kingston and his songstress Chynna James. That's when they would capitalize on the interest and let it be known that Lucas and Chynna had been carrying on an affair for some time. Fiona had also arranged after the tour stop for the next day for Lucas and Chynna to appear on several morning and talk shows and reveal their relationship.

Kenya was not looking forward to not only having to act like Chynna on tour, but act like she was Lucas's girlfriend as well. She was already walking a tightrope and had been doing a mighty fine job of it; but having to get close to Lucas was going to prove difficult if not impossible. She'd tried to push down the pulse of desire she'd felt when she was around him, had tried to act like it didn't exist, but it did. She was going to have to limit her close proximity to Lucas as much as humanly possible to avoid tipping her hand.

"Ready to slip into your dress?" Penelope asked.

Kenya looked into the mirror of her dressing room and blanched. She didn't recognize herself anymore. Staring back at her was this big-haired, overly made-up woman—in her opinion, a black Barbie doll.

"Looks great, right?" Derrick and Daisy said almost simultaneously.

"Uh ..." Kenya was at a loss for words, and before she could voice her concerns, they were shuffling her out of her robe and sliding the skintight dress over her head. It was clear that in Chynna's world she couldn't have qualms about showing her naked body as she was surrounded by people all the time.

Her assistant spun her around to face the mirror, and Kenya saw that she'd done it. She'd finally become Chynna.

KENYA CALMED her nerves later that evening as several of her bodyguards helped her into the oversized cake that she was to pop out of at the Beverly Wilshire hotel.

"When you hear the 'Happy Birthday' music, that's your cue to jump out, got it?" Deacon asked. Kenya had never seen him this excited at his and Fiona's handiwork.

Kenya nodded as she slinked inside the cake, then the guards covered her up with the cake top. She felt the cake being moved toward the ballroom where Lucas's party was already underway. She could hear the loud music and voices, but what struck her the most funny was that she'd hoped while she was living her twin's life that everyone would stop putting Chynna into a box. She'd hoped to show them her twin was more complex, but here she was being placed in a cake box to do their bidding.

Kenya knew in the long run that getting the paparazzi's focus off Blake and Chynna meant her sister could return to her life, but that didn't mean she had to like it.

Kenya heard the cue of the birthday music and instantly popped out of the cake. A spotlight shone on her with her big hair and made-up face as they wheeled her toward Lucas, who was sitting in a booth and watching in amazement as she seductively sang "Happy Birthday" to him. Her bodyguards surfaced to gingerly lift her out of the cake so she could slink her way toward Lucas and sit on his lap. Lucas played the devoted boyfriend and stared back at her as if he were enraptured by some mermaid singing in the ocean.

Kenya wasn't oblivious to the shocked stares of several party guests who had no idea that the two of them were an item. When she was finished with the song, she bent her head and gave the crowd something to cheer about. She swept her glossed lips across Lucas's. He lived up to his end of the bargain by sweeping his arms around her middle and kissing her firmly back. It was a short, but a somehow excruciatingly long kiss that made Kenya's toes curl in her stilettos.

When they pulled apart, Lucas's guests cheered in delight. "Guess it worked," he whispered in her ear.

"Guess so," she said for his ears only.

Soon Lucas's small table was besieged by several members of the press and partygoers. "Lucas, how long have you and Chynna been dating? Was this before or after Blake? Does Blake know that you and Chynna are seeing each other?"

"No comment." Lucas fanned the flames by not answering their pointed questions. "Let's dance." He helped Kenya to her feet then whisked her past the throng of onlookers toward the dance floor.

"You know, this is overkill," Kenya said softly as one of his hands grasped hers and the other was placed on the small of her back. "I think they all got we're an item."

Lucas pulled her firmly to himself and closed the distance between them. "We need to convince them we're legit so your movie gets back on track."

"I've already handled that," Kenya said as he smoothly danced her across the floor. She wasn't surprised that he was a good dancer. Lucas Kingston looked like the type of man who knew how to do everything well and not just dancing.

"Oh, yeah?" Lucas asked peering down at her. "And how'd you do that?"

Kenya heard the inflection in his voice and looked up at him. She ignored the butterflies that began to somersault in her belly and play havoc with her equilibrium. "I convinced Carter I had what it took to play Yvette."

"Really?"

"Don't sound so surprised."

"Well, from what I'd heard, you'd been struggling during rehearsals."

"I turned it around."

Lucas smiled, and Kenya noticed his straight, white teeth. They were too perfect. He had to have had some dental work done. She'd paid for hers thanks to her agent who'd insisted actors had to look great onscreen.

"Since you've been back, Chynna, you continue to both surprise and amaze me," Lucas admitted.

"I would hope that's a good thing."

"That remains to be seen," Lucas replied.

LUCAS WATCHED Chynna from across the room as she laughed and talked with several of his guests. The old Chynna he knew. She was gorgeous and sexy for sure, but she'd always been spoiled, impulsive and just a little bit needy. Since she'd returned from her two-week sabbatical at Canyon Ranch, she'd turned over a new leaf. She was just as drop-dead sexy as ever, but now, she was more vocal, deliberate and self-assured than she'd ever been. *Who is the real Chynna?* The dichotomy unnerved and perplexed him.

His nether regions had been on fire when he'd seen her pop out of that cake in that sexy lace dress. It seemed to have been poured onto her body and showed every generous curve, and he'd like nothing better than to run his fingers down each and every one. But since the song and the dance, they hadn't had one minute alone together. You'd think since they were supposed to be a couple that they'd be joined at the hip at the party, but everyone wanted to talk to her or be seen with her. He didn't see how she could stand all the incessant chatter, but she took photos and signed autographs with a smile because like it or not, Chynna was a seasoned professional.

Eli came up to him as he studied her. "She's something, isn't she?" he asked. "A real force that girl is. I told you when I signed her she'd be a star."

"And you're usually on the mark," Lucas replied.

"Usually," Eli said, looking at him strangely. "But nothing could have prepared me for the shock of seeing you and Chynna kissing."

"Oh, that," Lucas chuckled.

"Don't *oh, that*, my man," Eli replied. "Since when do you hold out on me about a woman, especially a *client*? I've never known you to mix business with pleasure, so what gives?"

Lucas shrugged. "She finally wore me down."

"Hmmpph."

"You know she's had a thing for me for a while."

"Yeah, but you never gave her the time of day," Eli

replied, swinging his glass back and taking a sip of his Hennessey and Coke.

"Well, I finally realized the error of my ways."

Eli stared at Chynna and then back at Lucas. "If that's how you want to play this, fine, Lucas. Just be careful. Chynna is our biggest star, and we wouldn't want anything to happen to this dynasty we've been building."

"Point taken." Lucas knew Eli was right, but it was like the pot calling the kettle black. Eli was always messing around with some of their lesser-named songbirds, but Lucas had never wanted to enter that arena until now. *Not until Chynna.*

EVENTUALLY THE CROWDS dissipated and Deacon and Fiona suggested that Lucas and Chynna leave together to give the press something to talk about. And talking they were.

As soon as Lucas and Kenya left the club, the paparazzi were clicking their cameras and trying to capture *the shot* as the couple entered the limo waiting at the end of the red carpet.

Kenya slid in first and Lucas was right behind her, but this time he sat opposite her. He immediately rolled up the partition window so the driver wouldn't hear their conversation.

"I am glad that's over," Kenya said, removing the stilettos from her aching feet and tossing them on the floor.

Lucas smiled. "You were great tonight. That happy birthday stunt was inspired. Whose idea was it?"

"Fiona's or Deacon's. I can't remember which."

"The paps are really going to eat this up," Lucas replied, eyeing them through the tinted limo windows.

"I sure hope so. I don't want have to keep this charade up too much longer."

"Why, When you're so good at it?"

"At what?"

"Acting like you're into me."

Kenya shrugged, trying to ignore the husky tone in his voice, but it was hard not to. "I told you I was working on my acting lessons."

"Hmm ... I don't think that was all acting," he said, watching her carefully.

Kenya tried to swallow, but her mouth suddenly felt parched. Lucas was staring at her so intently; there was no doubt in her mind of what was coming next. She just wasn't prepared for how strong her reaction would be when Lucas closed the distance between them.

He reached her seat and wrapped his large hands around her face and pulled her into a scorching kiss filled with so much heat, Kenya thought she might go up in flames. His lips hungrily caressed hers, coaxing them open, and Kenya parted her mouth to greedily accept his tongue.

Before she knew what was happening, Lucas was beside her and pulling her on top of him. His hands were everywhere, touching and caressing her arms, her hips, her butt and back up to mold her breasts with his big, strong hands while he made love to her with his tongue. His tongue thrust in and out of her mouth with an exquisiteness so delicious, Kenya molded the upper half of her body against his broad firm chest while the lower half began grinding against his erection.

"Chynna ..." Lucas's mouth left hers long enough to make its way up to her neck as he licked, kissed and caressed the sensitive part of her nape and ears. When he found she liked his ministrations, he continued teasing her earlobe and all her equilibrium crumbled.

"Oh God, yes," she murmured against his cheek, and he licked her earlobe and ground his bottom half against hers. But he didn't stop there. He pulled at the straps at the back of her corset until the thin lace fabric covering her breast could escape its confines and one chocolate nipple was his for the taking. That's when Lucas bent his head to suckle on her nipple. With gentle flicks of his tongue, he teased and licked the bud until it became erect. Then he moved to push down her bodice until her bosom was bare and he could feast on the other breast. He encircled her tender nipple with his tongue and Kenya felt herself becoming slick and wet inside her panties. She wiggled in his lap, wanting more.

Lucas must have sensed she was in a heat because she felt his hands exploring her butt and thighs long enough to start scrunching her dress upward until he reached the tiny scrap of fabric covering her femininity. When he found his destination, he pushed it aside so he could tease the slick folds of her womanhood with gentle fingers.

"Lucas ... please," Kenya began to pant, but that only seemed to fuel him, and he continued to surge forward, sliding one finger inside of her. She gasped as pure pleasure shot through her.

She began to buck against his thrusting and exploring finger, and Lucas whispered in her ear, "Yes, baby, come for me." He returned his mouth to hers and their tongues dueled for supremacy. Kenya felt she might come right there until she heard a knock on the limo door.

Startled, Kenya jumped away from Lucas to the opposite seat as if she'd been caught with her hand in the cookie jar. Lucas didn't know why when they were two consenting adults and he'd rather enjoyed what was happening between them.

"Mr. Kingston, we've arrived at Ms. James's estate," a male voice said from the other side of the door.

"Thank you. Give us a moment." Lucas stared across at Kenya, who was frantically pulling up her dress to cover those wonderfully full breasts of hers he'd been tantalizing. She seemed embarrassed at how wanton she'd behaved.

"Yes, sir."

"Perhaps we should take this inside?" he said.

"I, I don't think so," Kenya said breathlessly, fixing the bodice of her dress. "I think it's best if I go home *alone*."

"Excuse me?" Lucas was flabbergasted. They'd just been sharing one of the hottest moments he'd had with a woman since God knew how long and he was ready for the next logical step—the two of them making love until they were spent.

"I, I don't know what came over me," Kenya replied. "Th-that should have never happened and I need to go." She reached for the handle on the door, but Lucas grabbed her arms.

"Wait a second. Are you serious?" Lucas asked. "Are you honestly going to act like we weren't about to make love? Because I can assure you we were, and if we'd had another five minutes, I would've been buried deep inside you and you would have come."

He saw Chynna's fair skin color turn red. He hadn't meant to be so blunt, but he couldn't understand her change of heart. She clearly wanted him as much as he did her. That had been obvious by her unabashed response to him. So why was she backing away now when this was what she'd always wanted?

"You're right," Kenya said. "We would've had hot sex. But then what next? We have to carry on this charade for how long? You and I both know that you're not known for the long-term. So let's just chalk this up to me being a tease and call it a night, okay?"

Kenya didn't wait for a response. She escaped the confines of the limo before Lucas could stop her. He rolled down the window and watched her be escorted inside the mansion by one of her bodyguards as he sat with a major hard-on that would go unrequited for the night.

Damn that woman! She'd gotten him all worked up and *then* walked out on him. Maybe he'd been right about her all along. The problem was he'd already committed himself to a faux relationship to help clean up her image. Now what was he going to do? How the hell was he going to work with the woman he wanted to sex like crazy but who insisted on keeping him at arm's length?

9

"Hey, twinie," Chynna said into the receiver as she quietly called her sister from the study of the Hart estate the following evening. She'd waited until everyone had retired so she could make a private call.

"Chynna, oh thank God!" Kenya said from the other end. "How are you? I tried calling your cell, and then when I got no answer, I called the spa and they said they hadn't seen you in days and I was terrified something had happened to you. Where are you?"

"Well," Chynna sighed. "It's a long story."

"Spill it."

"I finally went for that hike you suggested and left my cell at the spa." Chynna glanced over her shoulder to make sure no one had entered the room. "And then I kind of got lost."

"Only you, twinie." Kenya laughed affectionately.

"I know, okay? Anyway, I stumbled onto this dude ranch."

"Dude ranch?"

"Yeah, the Golden Oaks Ranch is not far from the spa and they have cattle and horseback riding, skeet shooting, hay rides, a petting farm and all sorts of activities for families."

"And you're staying there?" Kenya sounded shocked by Chynna's choice of living quarters.

"Yes, I met the family that owns the ranch and they kind of took me in over the last week, so I need you to play me for just a little bit longer."

"How long?"

"That's it, Kenya. I don't know." Chynna just knew she had to stay and figure it out. "But what I do know is this is the most fun I've had since I can remember and this family is so warm and welcoming, especially Mrs. Hart. Makes me miss Mom."

"I miss her too, but I was hoping we could switch back. I thought this was only for a week or so and we would regroup after the Anaheim show."

"Is something wrong? Do you think someone's onto you?" Chynna sure hoped not.

"No, that's not it ..." Kenya paused for several seconds too long, and Chynna knew there was more to the story that her sister wasn't telling her.

"So what is it? Is it the Blake situation?" Chynna had hoped with time the press would move on to something new.

"No, I've handled that."

"Really? How?"

"Well, the press kind of, sort of ...thinks you and Lucas Kingston are an item."

"What!" Chynna rose from the executive chair she was seated in and began to pace the study room floor. "And why would they think that?"

"We all—being me, Deacon, Fiona and Lucas included—thought we needed to get the press's focus away from you and Blake and onto me, I mean you, and someone else. Since you'd always had a thing for

Lucas and he was single ... anyway, he agreed to take the heat so we could get the movie back on track. Carter Wright was ready to replace you."

"Wow! I can't believe Lucas would agree to stand in as my boyfriend, but he *did* think the movie was important. So how did it go? Am I out of the movie?"

"No, I gave the performance of my life by reading for Carter and I convinced him to keep you."

"And in return Lucas agreed to be your faux boyfriend?" Chynna sighed heavily. "Oh Lord, this is spinning out of control." When Kenya remained silent, Chynna knew there was more. "And, what else, twinie? What are you keeping from me?"

"I just really need to get back to my life," Kenya reiterated.

"Sounds to me like you want to run away." Chynna rubbed her chin and thought for a minute. "*Who* are you running away from?"

"Lucas and I, we became sort of intimate and it was such a stupid thing to do. It's why you need to get your butt back here and take your life back."

Chynna whispered into the phone, "How intimate did you and Lucas Kingston get?"

"Chynna!"

Chynna couldn't resist laughing because she could hear Kenya's discomfort over the phone. "I mean, I've been trying to hook that fish for years, but here you come and he gives up the goods. Oh, my—"

"Stop it." Kenya began laughing too, which helped ease the tension in her voice.

"You still didn't answer my question." Chynna wasn't jealous, not when she had Noah in her sights, but her curiosity was getting the best of her. "How far did you two go?"

"We didn't sleep together if that's what your insinuating."

Chynna sensed what her twin wouldn't say. "But you wanted to."

"I just think it's best if we switch places and return to our lives."

"No can do," Chynna said. "Like you, I've met someone too."

"Who?"

"Noah Hart. He runs his family's ranch. He tries to act like he's not interested in me, but I know men and he has the hots for me; but he won't admit it to himself. You see, he's a widower and he lost his wife and child very tragically and he's still suffering. I can't go. If I do, I'll never know if it's real, plus I told him I would stay on as a ranch hand for a couple of weeks, and I am determined to stick it out."

"Why? You have nothing to prove to him. He's a stranger."

"I have something to prove to me," Chynna said quietly. "That I'm stronger than everyone thinks and Noah ... well, he's just the icing on the cake."

"Icing on what cake?" a masculine voice said from behind Chynna.

Chynna wanted to die from embarrassment at having been caught talking about him. "I have to go," she whispered to Kenya. "I'll call you soon."

"When?"

"Soon." Chynna hung up the receiver and spun around to face Noah. He was looking as sexy as ever in his Wrangler jeans and plaid shirt. "Do you always eavesdrop?" she asked with indignation.

"Only if I hear my name," Noah said. "And what are you doing in here anyway?"

"I needed to make a private call."

"And you just happened to bring me up in the conversation?" Noah asked.

Chynna didn't have a quick retort, and Noah came rushing toward her and grabbed her by both shoulders.

"What's your game, Kenya?" He peered down at her. "Why are you here? Are you spying for one of our competitors?"

"Sp-spying?" Chynna managed to eke the word out because butterflies were fluttering in her belly at being this close to Noah again. "I, I have no idea what you're talking about."

She must have sounded genuine because Noah eased his firm grip on her arms, but he didn't release her. "Then what? Why are you here?" His words were barely a whisper as his mouth hovered over hers.

She knew he wanted to kiss her, so she said the words aloud that were hanging between them: "Kiss me."

Noah seemed shocked at her boldness and retreated momentarily, but he didn't let her go. He said instead, "I don't want to kiss you."

Chynna gave a wicked smile. "Liar. All this heat can't be coming just from me."

Before she could say another word, he pushed her backward against the door. Then he pulled her firmly into his arms, and her breasts brushed against his hard chest. She couldn't resist emitting a low moan, and that was the straw that broke Noah.

He lowered his head and pressed his lips against hers. He nibbled on her bottom lip until she parted her mouth. He plunged his tongue inside its warmth. His mouth settled over hers; the kiss was sweet, yet passionate. Noah kissed her like his life depended on it, like he couldn't get enough of her, and the feeling was mutual. Chynna couldn't ever remember being kissed in such a way. She allowed her hands to roam over his body. She reveled in the feel of the strong, corded muscles in his arms from so many days out on the ranch. The more Noah deepened the kiss, the more she felt weak at the knees and the more she knew that being intimate with this man was inevitable.

Noah felt like a randy teenage boy. Kenya tasted so good, felt so good. Rockets shot off in his head as he thrust his tongue deeper into her mouth. The frenzy of her movements, the moans escaping her lips, and the way her hips pushed and thrust against him made Noah want to slide his tongue between her legs and find out the secret within. He cupped her buttocks in his hands and pulled her firmly against his rock-hard erection.

She moaned again, and this time, his hands moved to roam over her hips, spine and then up to the slope of her breasts. He'd been dying to touch those sugary confections since he'd seem them in that tank top and shorts she'd worn a few mornings ago. Her breasts were full and ripe, and he rubbed her nipples until they turned into rocky pebbles. He wanted her anyway he could have her—on her back, on her knees, right here on the sheepskin rug in his father's study.

God, what's wrong with me? He was abandoning all of his principles and resolutions. Slowly, he pulled away from Kenya and took a large, uneven breath. "Th-that shouldn't have happened."

Or shouldn't it? He hadn't been with another woman since Maya's death. Maybe that was why he was reacting like he'd never been with a woman before, but deep in the back of his mind, he knew it wasn't true. Kenya was one of a kind, which is why he couldn't let this go on any further.

"If you ask me, that kiss was inevitable," Chynna said quietly as she tried to regain her composure

Curses fell from his mouth.

"Don't act like you didn't want it too," Chynna responded with a pout, "because I know otherwise."

Noah's face reddened. She was right. He'd been as hard as a rock kissing her. He still was. But he had to get his emotions under control.

"Listen, Noah," Chynna said, putting her hand up as he was about to speak again. "As much as you try to deny it, you're attracted to me. Why fight it?"

"Just give into the attraction?" he asked with a hoarse whisper.

"Why not?"

He didn't answer. Instead, he walked over to the wet bar and poured himself a drink of brown liquid from a decanter and sipped generously. When he finally spoke, he said, "In Hollywood, you might be used to casual sex, but I'm not." "When I make love to a woman, it's because she means something to me."

"And am I to interpret I mean nothing to you?"

"Well, uh ..." Noah was at a complete loss for words. The woman had a way of rattling him. "I, I didn't mean—"

"Ever the gentleman, Noah Hart." Chynna's eyes were alight with mirth. "I wouldn't dream of calling your honor into question."

Clearly, she'd seen how uneasy the question had made him and a wide grin curved his lips. "You were teasing me?"

She shared his smile. "I was because you, my friend, need to lighten up."

"And are you the woman to help me with that?" Noah inquired and took another sip of his drink.

Chynna shrugged. "Maybe. But for now, I'm going to leave you alone, Noah Hart." She walked toward the door, but paused to say, "But know that you and I," she said, pointing to him and back to herself, "are on a collision course and it's just a matter of time."

"A matter of time before what?" Noah asked, but the room was empty. The little minx had escaped, leaving him to wonder if she was right. Was it just a matter of time before they became lovers?

CHYNNA EXHALED DEEPLY as she closed the study door. She'd been surprised by Noah's response. She hadn't expected him to say something as honorable as, "When I make love to a woman, it's because she means something to me."

Then again, she'd never encountered a man quite like Noah Hart. He was a sexy cowboy who could wear a pair of jeans, but he was also a down-to-earth family man. *Is that the appeal? Am I attracted to him because he is so different from the Hollywood types?*

He was certainly different from Lamar and the other men she'd dated. Most were fame whores, hoping that by dating Chynna they could further their career. Sometimes it was hard knowing who she could trust much less give her heart to. So instead, she'd turned to sex. A quick romp between the sheets helped fill the need to be desired, to be touched by a man. But it was so fleeting, and most times, she ended up regretting those meaningless encounters. She hadn't been with as many men as the press made out, but she also wasn't by any means a virgin.

Why Noah Hart? There was something about him that told her innately that she could trust him, but there was also someplace deep inside that warned her to stay away because if she didn't, if she got too close to the sun, to this man, she would get burned.

Her resolve evaporated the next day when she was forced to ride horseback with Noah. It was barely six a.m. and they'd already been up, fed the horses, mounted them, and now, he was going to teach her how to help round up the cattle. There was nothing sexier than seeing a man, especially Noah, on horseback as he slapped his rope across his thigh and got the cattle and bulls to do his bidding. And when he roped a wayward steer, Chynna swallowed hard. She wondered what it would be like to have Noah roping her in as he rode her into oblivion.

"Kenya, Kenya!"

Chynna snapped herself out of her sinful daydream to the present to see Noah was down from his horse and looking up at her.

"Yes?"

"Do you intend on daydreaming all day or are you actually going to learn how to rope a steer?"

"Of course, I want to learn." She tried to get off the horse quickly but tumbled into Noah instead, and he had to catch her. He caught her by the shoulders to steady her and their eyes crossed for the merest of seconds, reminding her of the kiss they'd shared the night before. But he quickly moved away as if he didn't want to be near her.

"C'mon, I'll show you how it's done," Noah said and walked back to where several cattle were milling around, eating grass.

"Are you sure it's okay to be out here with them?" Chynna asked nervously, looking around at the large animals.

"Why? Are you afraid of another stampede?" Noah asked, laughing.

She pointed an accusatory finger at him. "Don't laugh. I could've been seriously injured when they tried to veer me off the road."

"Well you weren't and you'll be fine now," Noah replied, "because you have me."

Chynna raised a flirtatious eyebrow. "Do I? And you'll protect me?"

Noah didn't answer because another of the ranch hands came over to hand her some rope. He proceeded to show her how to tie the rope and demonstrated some lasso moves to help reel in the wayward cattle.

"Looks difficult."

"Takes practice," Noah replied. "But you'll get it. Come here." He wrapped his arms around her and attempted to show her again. But all she could focus on was his strong masculine scent.

Several hours later, Chynna was no better at tying the knot than she was at roping a steer, and it was even worse when Noah made her get on the horse's back to try it. But she refused to give up because she knew that's what Noah expected of her. She was happy when lunchtime blessedly came so she could give her sore bottom a break. Rylee hadn't been lying when she'd said that horseback riding for leisure was much easier than riding all day on a roundup.

Chynna returned her palomino to the stable for a rest and found Rylee in the stables tending to an injured horse.

"How's it going?" Chynna asked, poking her head

into the stall where Rylee was kneeling with her medicine bag.

Rylee glanced at a smudge-faced Chynna and replied, "I think I should be asking you that same question."

"It's going fine." Chynna tried to put on a happy face even though every muscle in her body ached.

"How's Noah treating you?" Rylee inquired, looking up from her task.

"Oh, he's fine."

Rylee stared at her suspiciously as if she didn't believe her. "Noah's been riding you pretty hard today. Are you sure you don't want to go back to the spa? Might be more fun."

Chynna shook her head. "No, believe it or not, this is the most fun I've had in ages."

"Then you must enjoy torture," Rylee replied. She'd always hated roundup and left it up to her brothers Noah and Caleb so she could tend to the animals.

Chynna laughed. "Guess I do."

"Unless there's some other reason." Rylee's brow rose.

"What do you mean?"

"C'mon, Chynna, I'm not blind, and I know my brother."

"And?"

"And I can't help but notice the way he looks at you," Rylee said. "I haven't seen that look in his eyes in years."

"You mean since Maya died?" Chynna had heard her name mentioned before, but knew precious little about her. She'd noticed his family seemed to be afraid to speak her name out loud so as to not offend Noah.

Rylee nodded.

"If you don't mind my asking, what happened?"

Rylee glanced around the stable. "I don't know if I should be telling you this."

"If you feel like you would be breaking Noah's confidence by telling me, then don't. You've been so good about keeping my secret, I wouldn't want to impose."

Rylee heaved a long sigh. "It's not that. Maya's death is such a sensitive topic with Noah. But ..." She paused. "If you're interested in my brother, you should know what you're up against."

"Interested in Noah?"

Rylee's incredulous look told Chynna she hadn't hidden her obvious interest in him. "Listen." She grabbed Chynna's arm and pulled her over to a nearby bench in the stall. "Maya was an amazing woman and loved by my entire family."

"Wow, you sure don't pull any punches."

"I want to be entirely transparent," Rylee said, "because it won't be easy to overcome the memory of her. She had a big place in this family. You see, she and Noah met when they were in the second grade. They'd known each other their entire lives, and it wasn't long before friendship turned to love. They were high school sweethearts, and when he went to college, she followed him. She'd wanted to start a family right away, but Noah had wanted to wait. He'd wanted to get his degree first and have time with just the two of them."

"What went wrong?"

"Fate. Maya found out she was pregnant and was so excited at the prospect of carrying Noah's child."

Telling the story was obviously taking a toll because tears began to well in Rylee's eyes. "I-I'd never seen my brother so over the moon. He was so ready to be a father. They'd decorated the baby's room at the house." She glanced up toward the main house. "Bu-but there ... there was a car accident. Maya was five months pregnant and ..." Rylee's voice choked, and she couldn't finish her sentence.

"And Maya and the baby didn't make it," a masculine voice said from behind them.

Startled, Chynna jumped up and saw Noah standing several feet away from her and Rylee. There wasn't a look of fury in his eyes that she would've expected; he just looked grief-stricken.

"I ..." Chynna was speechless. What could she ever say that would take away the pain of the fact that Noah had lost his wife and baby in one tragic swoop? It didn't seem fair.

Noah didn't say anything. Instead, he just turned on his heel and quietly left the stables.

"Oh Lord." Rylee's head sunk in her hands. "I should never have said anything."

Chynna rushed over to her side and rubbed Rylee's back. "Don't beat yourself up. You didn't do anything wrong. You just told me the truth. And from what I can see," she said, glancing at the empty doorway, "Noah's still not completely healed."

Rylee glanced up at Chynna with tear-stained cheeks. "Then, perhaps, it's time someone healed him."

"Me?" Chynna gave a nervous laugh. She didn't find the situation remotely funny, but she didn't know how else to react to such a bold statement.

"You're exactly what Noah needs to snap him out of his funk. You're a beautiful, glamorous, sexy spitfire and the exact opposite of Maya."

"Don't you think that perhaps that's the problem?

If you hadn't noticed, Noah's been doing an awfully good job at ignoring me."

"Don't let him." Rylee rose, then pushed Chynna toward the exit. "Go after him!"

Chynna's eyes widened in terror. "And what am I supposed to do?" Anything she could say would seem woefully inadequate.

Rylee wiped her cheeks with the back of her hand and smiled wanly. "You're Chynna James. I'm sure you'll figure it out. Go!" She pushed Chynna again toward the doorway.

With leaden feet, Chynna walked out of the stables and toward the main house. She wasn't sure what she was going to do when she found him or what Noah's reaction would be if she tried to break through the wall he'd erected around his heart. All she could do was try.

NOAH PACED HIS BEDROOM. He was fuming. He wasn't sure if he was angry with the fact that Rylee had betrayed him by revealing his secrets or the fact that Kenya knew he was damaged goods and might pity him. In any event, he was fit to be tied.

It wasn't Rylee's place to interfere and tell Kenya anything. His relationship and history with Maya was his and his alone. She had no right to tell Kenya about Maya's life *or death* for that matter. Hell, each time he thought he was closer to healing and getting over losing his wife and son, someone would tell the story again and fresh hurt would wash all over him in waves.

He couldn't handle that kind of sorrow anymore. The first time had nearly killed him. He hadn't known what was happening when he'd seen his father riding furiously toward him out in the meadow with the cattle. But once he'd approached, Noah had known something was wrong. The sheriff hadn't been able to reach Noah and had contacted the house to tell them that Maya had been injured in a car crash. He hadn't known how bad it was until he and his parents had made it to the hospital and the doctor had told him the grim news that the likelihood of Maya and the baby surviving while she was on a ventilator fighting for her life was slim-to-none. They'd been right and he'd lost them both within a matter of days.

He'd shattered in a million little pieces and retreated into himself for months. He hadn't left the house, but instead sat drinking alone in his room, cursing God for being so cruel. No one in the family could reach him, not Rylee, not even his mother. He'd been inconsolable. Eventually, it had been his father who'd knocked him into sobriety. He'd had enough of Noah wallowing in misery and had burst into his bedroom, grabbed him by the collar, and hauled Noah in his drunken stupor into the shower. He'd been fully clothed, but the cold shower had sobered him up. He and his father had a long talk, and eventually, he'd let out the tears that he'd bottled up inside for months and slowly began to move on.

"Noah?" A gentle knock sounded on his door. Noah didn't have to answer to know who it was. He could *sense* her presence before she entered his room. And she did, without waiting for an invitation.

"Go away!" He stood resolutely, looking out the window across the fields. He hadn't asked Kenya to follow him. Why couldn't she leave him in peace with his thoughts, his memories of the past?

"That's not going to happen," Kenya said, and he

heard her soft footsteps approaching him from behind.

He sucked in a breath when he felt her hands touch his arm. "Noah, please."

He refused to look at her and kept his back turned. "I don't want to talk about this, Kenya."

"Perhaps you should. Perhaps it's time to start letting go of the hurt."

With that comment, he spun around and away from her. "Let go. Why? So you and I can start something?"

"Maybe, maybe not." She shrugged. "But you can't go on like this. You're a raw nerve right now, and you've got to let someone in sometime."

"I don't have to do a goddamn thing. You know nothing about her!" he said through gritted teeth.

Her eyes were hazy with tears. Or was it pity? "Do you think Maya would want this empty life for you? Don't you think she would want you to move on with your life and be happy?"

Noah was amazed at her gall. "How dare you talk about her."

"Why? Because I'm not fit to speak of her?" Kenya challenged him. "Because I wouldn't live up to her memory? Well, you're right, Noah Hart. I'm never going to be your late wife. But the fact of the matter is, she's gone."

"And you're here?" he spat at her, and within seconds, he'd closed the distance between them. "Well, if you're offering yourself to salve my wounds, then by all means, let's get it on." He knew the words were crass as he said them and hated himself for being such a jerk, but he seemed powerless to stop himself.

When he reached her, she took several steps away, but in so doing, she lost her footing and fell back against the bed. *How apropos*, Noah thought. She was the sexiest creature he'd ever encountered and maybe it was time to see if she was as good as the package she presented.

She must have sensed the dangerous look in his eyes because she backed away from him on the king-sized bed, but that only secured her place in his lair. "Noah, listen. I know you're upset now. So perhaps we should talk about this—"

But before she could finish her sentence, he'd pounced and was beside her on the bed. "You want to make it better for me," Noah hissed, shrugging out of his lambskin leather coat and tossing it to the floor. "Well, you can do that right here and right now. Make me forget about my former life, Kenya."

He lowered his body onto hers, and his hands captured her face so his mouth could seek hers. And when he found it, he wasted no time thrusting his tongue inside. *Damn those bee-stung lips of hers.* They were so deliciously soft and sweet that he nibbled at her lower lip, and she moaned underneath him like the sweet thing she was. Then she wrapped her arms around his neck and kissed him back as fiercely as he'd kissed her.

He'd meant the kiss to be punishing, to make Kenya realize that she could never compete with Maya, and that all she would be good for was a romp in the hay. The problem was the moment his mouth had touched hers, he'd sparked a fire and a slow burn began to course through him. His tongue became less urgent, and he allowed himself to ever so slowly explore the inner crevices of her mouth while his hands roamed over her soft, supple body.

Kenya didn't fight his caresses. When his hands brushed the swell of her breasts and the curve of her hip, she leaned into him as if she too were desperate for more. His animal nature seemed to take over and touching her was not enough—he wanted to taste her. He pulled the plaid shirt from the waistband of her jeans and nearly ripped it off her shoulders.

When her shirt was open, he feasted his eyes on her beautiful breasts in the lace demi bra she wore. If he'd known she'd barely been wearing anything underneath that shirt, he might have done this sooner. But instead, he cupped one breast in his hands and lowered his head so he could finally have a taste. His tongue feverishly licked her nipple through the lace of her bra. When she gave a little purr, he nearly became undone. He pushed aside the scrape of fabric and tugged at the turgid peak with his teeth. She writhed underneath him, so he treated the other breast to the same licking and lapping treatment.

If he hadn't heard his mother calling him—"Noah, Noah? Are you up here?" —he would have put his hands down her jeans to touch the place he was sure was wet from the way she'd been moving underneath him. There wasn't a shadow of doubt in his mind that he would have taken Kenya right there on his bed in the middle of the afternoon.

Noah became still above Kenya and didn't move a muscle. When his mother didn't hear his response, she must have given up because he heard footsteps moving away from his door.

"Damn!" He shouted the obscenity as he quickly jumped away from Kenya and sat his feet firmly on the ground. Disgusted by his behavior, he grasped his head in his hands and lowered his head.

Kenya didn't say a word as she buttoned what was left of the shirt he'd nearly ripped off and scooted off his bed.

She stood in front of him now, and Noah wanted to apologize, but there was no excuse for how abominably he'd behaved. He'd never treated a woman with such disrespect in his life, and he couldn't fathom why he'd started now. *What was it about Kenya that caused him to react irrationally?*

"If you think you can use me like a whore to erase the memory of your dead wife, you are sorely mistaken, Noah Hart," Kenya said. "Don't come near me again!"

And without another word, she slammed out of his bedroom.

10

"You ready to do this?" Deacon said when he popped his head into Chynna's dressing room later that evening. They were at the Honda Center in Anaheim, California, for Chynna's first concert since news of her and Blake's supposed affair broke out over a month ago.

Kenya nodded. She still couldn't believe that in less than half an hour, she was going to be on stage in front of thousands of people. Sure, she knew all the songs and now with hours and hours of practice had most of Chynna's dance moves down, but it seemed so surreal.

Just a few weeks ago, she'd been living a ho-hum life in New York, waiting to hear if her critically acclaimed dramedy would be picked up for another season, and now, here she was in Hollywood living her *sister's life*! How things could change on a dime. But the funny thing about all of this was of all the parts she'd been asked to play, she was *made* for this one. Who knew Chynna better than her? Who had powerhouse singing chops like Chynna? And most of all, who had Chynna's face when they stared in the mirror? Kenya.

Convincing Chynna's adoring public, however, that she was still the same diva they'd all come to love would be difficult. But Kenya had always known she was born to act, and this time would be no different. She would go out there tonight and give it her all.

"Yes, I am," Kenya said authoritatively as she stood up in a bondage outfit. She'd tried her best to pare down the sexy image, but the costume designer insisted she knew what would look best on stage.

Kenya, on the other hand, just hoped that her breasts didn't pop out from the leather bandages of the mini-dress, paired with fishnet stockings and stilettos, she wearing. She'd hated the collar of the dress that wrapped around her neck because it reminded her of a dog collar, not to mention the dress left very little to the imagination.

She inhaled a deep breath and marched out of the room. She found her dancers and the band waiting for her in the hall.

"Chynna," Deacon said.

She stared at him and the rest of the group blankly for several minutes. It didn't help that when she glanced up, she saw Lucas and Eli walking toward them. She had avoided Lucas since that night in the limo when they'd almost made love. He must have felt the same and been furious with her for leading him on because he hadn't shown up to her dance practice or contacted her staff in days. Seeing him now did little to alleviate her tension. Instead, she felt more wound up than ever.

"Aren't you going to say something?" Eric, one of her dancers, asked. He was the one with whom Chynna had had a one-night stand.

That's when Kenya remembered what Chynna told her—that she'd always said a prayer before going out on stage. "Let's bow our heads, everyone." She lowered her head and grasped one of her female dancer's hands. "Lord, please be with us tonight as we perform in front of the good people of Anaheim. Help us have a great show and entertain the masses in Jesus's name, Amen."

"Amen," they all said when the prayer was over.

"Let's go out there and give it our all," she yelled. There were lots of hoots and hollers as the group began walking toward the back of the stage.

"Chynna, a word." Lucas grabbed her by the arm and pulled her away from the group.

"Yes?" She raised a quizzical brow.

His eyes assessed hers frankly as if he wanted to say something, but thought better of it. She did, however, catch his roving eye over her body, which hadn't missed an inch of the bondage dress she was wearing.

When he was finished, she asked, "You like?"

"Absolutely." He stunned her by brushing his lips softly across hers and smacking her on the bottom. "Go knock 'em dead, baby!"

His actions were not missed by the band or the dancing troupe and several of them hooted and hollered again.

Two hours later, sweating and delirious from the cheers and yells of Chynna's screaming fans, Kenya made her way down the hall to her dressing room after accepting a towel from security to wipe the sweat away.

She'd done it! She'd given the performance of her life and convinced them all that *she* was Chynna James. She couldn't resist going over to the ice bucket where champagne was chilling and popping off the top. She couldn't wait for someone to do it for her.

That's how Deacon found her, swigging champagne straight from the bottle. This kind of fame was heady and could totally be addictive. Kenya threw back her head and took another swig of champagne.

"What's gotten into you?" Deacon asked, laughing as he closed the door.

"Oh, I don't know," Kenya said, smiling, her voice rising slightly as she spoke. "Wasn't that an awesome concert?"

"Hell, yeah," Deacon said, taking the champagne bottle from her and taking a swig himself. "I haven't seen you that energized in years."

Kenya paused for a moment to study him. "Really? Why would you say that?"

Deacon shrugged. "Oh, I don't know. Guess you had kind of lost the joy of it all recently. But tonight, tonight you were on fire. I haven't seen you like that before. It was infectious!"

Kenya broke into a wide-open smile at the compliment. "Thank you. I was feeling it."

"And the crowd sensed it," Deacon said. "When you came back out for the last song, I thought they were going to tear the stadium apart."

"Do you really think so?" Kenya asked hopefully. She'd given the show her all and had never felt better. She felt like she was on top of the world. *Invincible.*

"THAT WAS ONE HELLUVA SHOW, HUH?" Lucas commented to Eli as they left the skybox where they had VIP seats to watch the concert.

"Yeah, it was pretty cool," Eli said, rubbing his chin.

"Why don't you sound more hyped?" Lucas asked. "Chynna gave a great performance. The fans were on their feet nearly the whole show."

"Oh, yeah, man, I'm not saying she didn't do a fantastic job."

"What then?" Lucas noticed that Eli appeared deep in thought.

"Oh, I don't know," Eli said. "There was just something different about her tonight."

"She was on fire is what she was!"

"No doubt. No doubt."

Lucas didn't like the tone in Eli's voice. "Is something wrong?"

"No, it's just that our girl Chynna seems different somehow, and I just have to figure out why that is."

"Why, when she's doing so great? Ever since she got back from the spa, she's been rejuvenated. Clearly, the time away was exactly what she needed."

"Yeah, you must be right," Eli replied, but in the back of his mind, he wasn't so sure. Lucas was right about one thing though: Since she'd gotten back from Arizona, Chynna *had* been a changed woman, and it wasn't that he didn't appreciate her renewed interest in her career, but she was much more vocal and he preferred his artists to be seen and not heard. If Chynna continued in this vein, Eli wasn't sure he could convince her to do things his way.

KENYA LET the hot shower run over her body the following morning. The pulsating water was exactly what she needed to prepare her for the day ahead. Last night's concert had been exhilarating, but afterward, she'd had to board a red-eye flight to New York. She was exhausted, which didn't bode well for the day, given that today would test every one of her acting abilities. Today, she and Lucas were going to set the record straight by appearing on *Good Morning America* and *Live with Kelly and Michael* to talk about their relationship, then back to California for their final appearance on *Ellen.*

The press had besieged her mansion and R&K Record's offices since Lucas's birthday party several nights ago. They were desperate for any shred of information about the new darling Hollywood couple: When did the relationship begin? What was their first date? Where did they go? Endless questions were being thrown at her each day, but she'd remained mum per Fiona's instructions. By not revealing any info, the paparazzi had been lathered into a fever pitch. The plus side was that she and Blake were no longer the main topic of conversation. Hallelujah!

As she soaped her body with the loofah sponge, she couldn't get Lucas Kingston out of her mind. And as the sponge touched that sensitive part of her flesh, her mind instantly wandered to the moment Lucas's hand had been under her dress in the limo, and the fevered pitch he'd brought her to. He'd been right about one thing: If that car ride had taken longer, she would've succumbed and had sex with him in the back of the limo and then what would he think of Chynna?

Despite her wanton behavior that night, Kenya felt that over the last week, he'd begrudgingly given her some props for standing up to him and her team. But she also didn't want to take two steps back in his mind and have him think of her as a floozy he could sex on the backseat of his limo. *If* she let him take her to bed, and that was a big *if*, he'd have to romance her. Kenya stood under the showerhead, and the suds slowly eased off her body. Being so close to Lucas today would not be easy, but she was determined that he would treat her with respect.

When she'd done showering, she wrapped a fluffy bath towel around her body and exited the bathroom. She found Megan had already taken the liberty of taking out a sleeveless, cream-colored sheath with matching pumps for her to wear on camera. Several other outfits were laid out for her to take for the other guest appearances. Apparently, she couldn't be seen in the same outfit on a different show.

Kenya sighed. Now, she could see how Chynna could get weary of everyone making decisions for her every day.

She'd been nearly done dressing and spritzing her wrists with perfume when she heard a knock on the door. "Come in."

It was Fiona. "Are you ready?"

"Of course, Fiona," Kenya said testily. "I'm a pro."

"I'm sorry, Chynna, I didn't mean ...," Fiona began, but Kenya walked toward the other woman and patted her hand.

"I'm sorry," Kenya replied. "I shouldn't have jumped down your throat." It wasn't Fiona's fault that she was about to be bound to Lucas Kingston for the next few hours.

"I just wanted to let you know the limo has arrived to take you and Lucas to your first interview, on *Good Morning America*."

Kenya's stomach churned over in knots at the mention of Lucas. They hadn't been alone since that night, and today they'd have to pull off that they were a couple newly in love.

"Thanks, Fiona." Kenya smiled back at her publicist. "You've done a great job at putting this press tour together on short notice. I promise I'll nail this."

Deacon and Fiona accompanied Lucas and Kenya fifteen minutes later in the limo and chattered on so incessantly about what they should say and how they should react, that Kenya had no time to be nervous.

Lucas had remained quiet for most of the drive until he'd finally said, "I think we get it, Fiona," effectively shutting up the frazzled publicist. He seemed to be as much on edge as Kenya.

Kenya fiddled with the clutch in her lap, desperate for something to do so she wouldn't have to look at him. She pulled out her lip gloss to touch up her mouth, and when she did, she found Lucas staring at her intently from across the limo. Her throat began to feel dry from his scorching gaze. "Fiona, pass me a bottled water, would you?"

Fiona pulled an Evian from the small fridge in the inside of the limo and handed it to Kenya. Kenya quickly unscrewed the top and took a long gulp.

The limo came to a sudden stop, and Kenya heard fans calling Chynna's name, which indicated they'd made it to their destination. Several bodyguards came around from the front seat to escort Chynna and Lucas from the limo with Deacon and Fiona following in close pursuit.

Kenya signed autographs and took a picture with a fan before she was hustled inside the studio toward the greenroom. She walked inside, followed by Lucas, who stopped Deacon and Fiona from entering at the doorway.

"Why don't you give Chynna and me some time alone, eh?" he asked, but Kenya knew he wasn't really asking. He was *telling* them he wanted to talk to her *alone*.

"Sure thing, Lucas. We'll be around." Deacon glanced at Kenya, who nodded her assent from behind Lucas.

Lucas closed the door behind him and turned to

face Kenya. She stepped backward and folded her arms across her chest.

"Chynna, please." Lucas gave an exaggerated sigh. "I'm not about to attack you."

"I know that," she said defensively.

"You could have fooled me," Lucas replied as he walked toward her. "In the limo, you were like a tiger ready to attack if I made one move toward you. And given what we're about to try and pull off today, that's not going to work."

Kenya inhaled sharply. He had a point. She had to get over her skittishness because they were about to act like they were an adoring couple. "You're right. So what do you suggest we do about it?"

"This." One of Lucas's hands reached across the short distance between them and pulled her by the neck until she was inches away.

Kenya closed her eyes, ready for some sort of attack, but instead, Lucas gently brushed his lips across hers. Her eyes fluttered open just as he deepened the kiss, and his tongue surged inside her mouth to collide with hers. They mated together as one, tasting and devouring each other. His other hand caressed her hair, cheek, and the curve of her hip, bringing her closer to him until her breasts were pressed firmly against his chest.

Sparks grew, but instead of taking the kiss further, Lucas pulled away.

Kenya stared at Lucas blankly. "Why did you do that?"

"Kiss you?" he said. "Because I needed you to have *that look* in your eye."

"What look?" Kenya turned to stare at herself in the mirror but couldn't see anything different other than her smudged lip gloss, which would need repair.

"The look you have right now that says you want me," Lucas said. "It will play well to the camera."

Kenya opened her mouth to say something, but nothing came out.

"We have to convince the public that we're the real deal," Lucas said. "And we couldn't do that if you're scared for me to touch you. Now you're more relaxed."

Kenya felt anything other than relaxed. She felt like a cat on a hot tin roof. Lucas hadn't kissed her because he'd wanted to. He'd done it so he could heighten her awareness of him to play up to the interview. And it had worked. She was very *aware* of him.

Lucas opened the door to the greenroom and allowed Deacon, Fiona, Derrick and Daisy in. They immediately ushered her into a seat.

"What happened to your lips?" Daisy asked as she set about touching up her makeup.

Kenya glanced up to find Deacon smiling knowingly at her, but he didn't comment on how her lip gloss had gotten smudged even though Lucas had a hint of sheen on his lips.

THE INTERVIEWS on all of the shows went well. Kenya was surprised at just how good an actor Lucas really was. He acted like an adoring new boyfriend who couldn't get enough of Chynna. He had one hand around her shoulder and the other held one of hers. And several times during each interview, he'd leaned over to give her a quick kiss on the cheek. He was so good at it that if Kenya didn't know otherwise, she would believe he was a man in love. *Is this what Lucas does with the women he dates? Does he make them believe he is in love before he dumps them?*

"I'm glad that's over," Lucas said when they were on the plane heading back to Los Angeles.

"You guys did fantastic!" Fiona gushed. "You were really convincing."

"A little too convincing," Deacon muttered underneath his breath.

"What was that?" Kenya said from beside him.

"Oh, nothing," Deacon replied. "Great job!"

"Good," Lucas said. "Now Chynna can focus on the movie without fear of the press hounding her about Blake."

"You know this isn't the end," Fiona replied. "We'll still need the two of you to go out on a few *public* dates before we can release that the two of you broke up."

"That won't be a problem," Lucas replied.

"Excellent!" Fiona was happy with her handiwork, but Kenya was not looking forward to spending more time in Lucas's company. Today had shown her that Lucas had a way with women— he'd easily made putty of her today in the greenroom after all. If he really put on the charm, just how long would she be able to resist it?

KENYA WAS nervous as she sat in her trailer a couple of days later. Daisy was making her up for one of the first scenes she would film with Blake. Her whole team had come to the set, but Kenya would have preferred quiet so she could run her lines again in her head. It was imperative that she not screw this up. Chynna was depending on her to pull through some of these scenes. Since they were filming out of order, some of the more dramatic scenes would be taped in advance. Thankfully, when Chynna returned, she'd have less acting to deal with because Kenya would do all the heavy lifting.

What didn't go so well was her wardrobe fitting. The film's wardrobe had already been selected weeks ago when Chynna had been fitted. Unfortunately, Kenya was an inch or so larger in the midriff than Chynna, and the costume designer wasted no time making a point of the weight gain.

"She needs to lose five pounds," the designer said, glancing over at Deacon as if Kenya wasn't in the room.

"I'll take care of it," Deacon said.

Kenya glared at Deacon as the woman rushed off to let out the snug-fitting mini-dress. *He will take care of it? He isn't the boss of me.*

Deacon must have sensed her fury, because he said, "No carbs. We've done this before, Chynna. You know how the camera adds fifteen pounds. It'll be fine." He patted her shoulder as if she were an inconsolable child.

Kenya hated being patronized and shrugged him off. "Take a break. I need some privacy."

"Chynna ...," Deacon began, but Kenya held up her hand.

"Out." She pushed him toward the trailer door.

When they'd all blessedly left, Kenya sighed. *How am I going to pull this off?* Had anyone noticed the difference in her figure versus Chynna's? Five pounds? It was closer to ten. Although she wasn't fat by any means, she was much more athletic than Chynna and muscle weighed more. She was going to have to starve herself to fit in that skinny outfit.

Kenya needed to talk to someone. She reached for her purse and called her twin, but her cell phone rang and rang, so Kenya finally gave up. She was going to have to get through this on her own. But how? She'd never done a motion picture before. Television was different. They had all the time in the world to tape, but film moved much quicker. *What if I tank?*

Her cell phone rang and Kenya tapped the screen, hoping it was Chynna. It wasn't.

"Chynna." It was Lucas. *What is he doing calling me?*

"What do you want?"

"Well, I was hoping I could come in, but I was told you'd kicked everyone out for privacy."

"Come in?"

"I'm outside the trailer," Lucas said. "Figured I couldn't not show up to support my girlfriend's first day filming. What would the press think?"

He is entirely too good at this, Kenya thought as she stepped down to open the trailer door. Lucas was standing outside in the sunlight, looking good enough to eat. He looked fresh-shaven and was wearing a collared navy-colored jersey sweater and some jeans. Kenya couldn't remember ever seeing Lucas wear jeans. The casual look was good on him.

"May I?" he asked, motioning toward the door.

"Come in," she said. She glanced at Deacon outside her door and pointed at him. "Not a word." She knew he suspected there was more going on to her and Lucas's relationship, but as her manager, he was the epitome of discretion.

Lucas brushed past her on the steps as he walked up the trailer, and her nipples instantly hardened. God, what was wrong with her? Whenever she was around this man, she became horny as hell.

Slowly, she walked up the steps and found that having Lucas in her small trailer made it feel dwarfed. He sucked up all the air in the room, and it disoriented her. Not to mention those jeans accentuated his tight butt.

"How do you feel?" Lucas asked, staring at her.

"Hmm? Oh, I'm fine."

"Liar," he said, taking a seat on the couch. "You look tense. I thought you said you had this."

Kenya straightened her back. "I do. But this is my first movie, in case you've forgotten."

"I haven't," Lucas said, watching her intently. "I just have faith in you that you can do this."

"Thanks," Kenya said as she tugged at the too-small top she was wearing and pulled it down over her midriff. She couldn't wait for the replacement top to be let out.

Lucas's eyes caught the action and did a slow roam over her outfit. "A little snug?"

Kenya rolled her eyes and frowned. "Don't remind me. I was told to lose a few pounds." She reached for a bottle of Evian she'd opened earlier, and she sipped.

"I kind of like the extra pounds," Lucas said. "Gives me more to hold on to."

Kenya swallowed hard. There was no mistaking the sexual innuendo in that statement. She tried to ignore him by changing subjects and bringing up the public date Fiona wanted to arrange for them at Spago at the Hotel Bel-Air. It was easier than focusing on the obvious sexual tension between the two of them.

Kenya glanced around for something to use to fan herself. *When did it get so hot in the trailer?*

LUCAS NOTICED Chynna's obvious agitation as she moved around the small trailer. He'd thought it was nerves about the movie, but then he thought better of it and rose from the small sofa and walked over to her at the counter.

When she turned around, he was right behind her and consequently, had her backed in a corner between him and the counter. "Why does being around me make you so uncomfortable?" Lucas inquired, raising a brow. "Before you left for Tucson, you wanted more between us, and now that it's here ..." His voice trailed off. He couldn't put his finger on it, but there was definitely something different about Chynna.

She tried to stand up straight, but by doing so, her breasts puckered out in the skimpy top she wore, and Lucas couldn't resist staring at them in all their beautiful perfection. The memory of tasting those sweet chocolate morsels came to him, and he could feel himself hardening.

"I-I'm not uncomfortable," Kenya said.

Lucas wanted to call her bluff, but he knew she needed to be on set soon. So he didn't want to start something he wouldn't be able to finish.

"Good." Lucas pushed away from her and heard her audible sigh of relief. "I just wanted to say, break a leg on set today."

"Thanks."

As he drove back to R&K Record's offices, Lucas was sure of one thing: There was no denying that the attraction between the two of them was real and very potent. Every time they were together, the air crackled with unrequited lust. No matter how much Chynna tried to resist it, they were going to become lovers. There was no doubt in his mind.

11

Staying away from Kenya was damn near impossible, given she was a guest in his family's house, but Noah had tried his best to honor her wishes after he'd behaved so terribly toward her a couple of days ago. He'd made sure Jonas showed her the ropes on the ranch. At times, he would catch her outside hauling hay, cleaning stalls and trying her best to rope in the steers, but he kept his distance. Even at dinner, he acknowledged her presence and was polite when spoken to, but nothing more.

He knew his parents and Rylee had to be wondering what was going on between them, which is why it was no surprise when Rylee confronted him two days after the incident.

"Okay, what gives?" his little sister asked him at the check-in desk at the lodge as new guests were arriving.

"What do you mean?" Noah asked, even though he knew *exactly* what she was referring to. He left the desk to go to the back of the house, where they would not be heard.

"What's going on between you and Ch-I mean Kenya," Rylee whispered as they walked into the management office. "And don't say 'nothing' because I know better."

"I don't want to discuss this with you."

"Is that so?" Rylee said, following behind him and shutting his door. "Well, I disagree. The two of you have been so damn polite to each other, I want to scream. Tell me what happened."

Noah's eyes darkened when he turned to his sister. "This is none of your affair, Rylee. Stay out of this."

"Affair?" Rylee noticed his choice of words. "Is that what's going on? Did you have a lover's spat?"

"Of course not!" Noah responded. "How could you think that?"

"C'mon, Noah, I'm not a little kid anymore," Rylee said. "And I can see with my own two eyes that there's something between you and Kenya."

"You're wrong."

"And you're fooling yourself, big brother. You've got a beautiful woman who's obviously interested in you. What would be so wrong with spending time with her and enjoying life? Haven't you suffered enough?"

"Don't start, Rylee."

"I know Maya wouldn't have wanted you to be celibate and live like a monk."

"Rylee Hart!" He stared at her in disbelief. He couldn't believe his little sister's audacity.

Rylee smiled coquettishly. "What? Do you think I live like one?"

Noah covered his hands with his ears. "I don't want to hear this."

"That what? Your little sister has a sex life?" Rylee asked with her hands on her hips. "Well, I do. And I'm not afraid to say it. Perhaps you shouldn't be afraid of one either."

"I'm not afraid."

"Bullshit!" Rylee said. "And I'm telling you that you need to do something about it."

"Like what?"

"Well, we have our thirty-fifth anniversary party this weekend. You should invite Kenya as your date."

"I don't think that's a good idea." Plus, he suspected she would say no. Why would she choose to spend her time with a man who'd behaved so boorishly? If Maya could see him now, she'd be embarrassed at the way he'd treated another woman. But he hadn't a clue as to how to make it up to Kenya. *What could I say? That I'd lost my mind temporarily?*

"Why not invite her?"

He decided to be honest. If nothing else, it would get Rylee off his back. "Kenya and I had a disagreement, so I doubt she would want to spend time with me of her own free will."

"Well, you won't know that unless you ask her."

"You want me to put myself out there? What if she says no?"

"I have a feeling you might be surprised by her answer if an apology is offered with the invitation. But you'll never know if you don't try."

Seconds later, she'd walked off, leaving Noah to his own thoughts. *Is Rylee right? Could Kenya forgive me and agree to attend the party with me?*

He was torn. He wanted to make amends, and the truth of the matter was he did want to get to know Kenya better, but he couldn't remember the last time he'd asked a woman out. It had to have been in his teens, before he'd seen Maya blossom and he realized she was the woman he wanted to spend the rest of his life with.

But she was gone. He was still here. Somehow, he

had to find a way to move on with his life. Kenya had been right when she'd called him out on it. Perhaps that's why he'd gotten so upset? Regardless, he needed to make things right with Kenya, whether she agreed to be his date to the party. He wouldn't want her to leave the ranch remembering him as the guy who'd treated her so miserably.

Noah smiled inwardly. Somehow Kenya having a good opinion of him was extremely important. In a short time, she had broken through the barrier he'd had up. The question was, would he finally allow her to enter?

CHYNNA WAS BRUSHING the baby colt that Rylee had delivered earlier that morning. She'd been awed by the sight of seeing the colt being born. She'd never seen anything in her life like it and doubted she ever would again. Being on the ranch had opened her eyes to so many new experiences. She'd found she was capable of a lot more than she'd thought. *Who would have figured I could haul hay, clean up a stall or milk a cow for that matter?*

Milking the cow had been a hilarious experience as the cow had kicked over the bucket and the milk in the pail had splashed all over her. Then there was helping the ranch crew and the entire Hart family prepare for their big thirty-fifth celebration. She'd hung streamers and lights, moved furniture and generally pitched in where needed. When Madelyn had asked for her help in the kitchen, initially Chynna had been reluctant. She'd never cooked a day in her life, but she'd been in the kitchen with Madelyn, rolling out dough for pies and, of course, getting it all wrong.

But at least she would have all the memories of

her experiences here once she went back to the real world and picked up her life as the infamous pop star Chynna James. She knew her time on the ranch would have to come to an end soon. Kenya couldn't and wouldn't live her life indefinitely, though Chynna suspected she was enjoying her time with a certain handsome music mogul. Chynna just wished there would've been time to see what was between her and Noah.

He was a hard man to figure out. On the one hand, he was a dedicated rancher and family man, but on the other, he was a tortured soul, living under the shadow of his dead wife's memory. Despite how strong he appeared on the outside, he couldn't seem to let her go.

She'd tried to reach out to Noah, and her efforts had her ending up in his bed, but not in the way she imagined. For a moment, he'd lost himself and wanted to forget his wife and had used Chynna as an outlet. Chynna had forgiven him after it had happened because she could see he was so tortured. She would have talked with him about the incident sooner, but he'd seemed so intent on not forgiving himself, that she'd let it go and kept her distance.

Of course, the reason she'd done that hadn't been merely for his benefit. Her reaction to him had scared her. He'd been tortured, but what was her excuse for giving into him so freely? When he'd first kissed her, it had been out of anger, but then it had changed. There had been passion lying underneath the surface and she'd succumbed. She'd let him touch her, suckle her. She hadn't been able to shake the memory of his lips on her breasts and how it had made her feel. Her insides had liquefied, and if his mother hadn't called out his name, she was sure she would've allowed him to make love to her. And it would have been wrong because it wouldn't have been for the right reasons. At least not for him, and he would have regretted the encounter and despised her. Thankfully, fate had intervened.

But it still didn't change the fact that Chynna still wanted Noah Hart. But did he want her? Really want her and not as a substitute or warm body that could help him forget his dead wife?

"Kenya, do you have a moment?"

The object of her desire, looking tan, sexy, and wearing a pair of Wranglers, was standing in the doorway to the stall.

"Yes?"

Noah stared at his feet and shifted uncomfortably.

"What is it?"

"I was hoping we could take a ride, maybe have some lunch?" Noah asked uneasily. "So we could talk."

Chynna put down the brush she'd been using. To talk was all she'd wanted to do the last couple of days. She hadn't wanted this distance between them, not when she sensed she was close to breaking through the barrier he'd erected around his heart. "A ride sounds good."

Thirty minutes later, after they'd saddled up the horses with a blanket and a small picnic basket, Noah took them on a short ride past the lake, where they had airboat rides for the guests, to a small pond that featured a dazzling water fountain. Once they'd dismounted and Noah had tied up his Arabian and her palomino, he pulled out the blanket and untied the picnic basket from his horse's saddle.

"C'mon." He grabbed her hand again and her heart turned over. She didn't know why she felt like a schoolgirl around him, but she did. She accepted the hand he offered and walked with him toward the pond's edge. It was a quiet, secluded area on the ranch property that their guests knew nothing about. It was a setting made for lovers, and Chynna relished the opportunity to spend time alone with Noah, but they were also about to have their first *serious* talk.

Once he'd found an advantageous spot, he put down the picnic basket. Then he shook out the blanket, spread it on the grass and lowered himself to the ground. He held out his hand so he could help Chynna down onto the soft blanket that felt like chenille or maybe cashmere.

"This outing is quite unexpected," Chynna replied, watching him carefully. She felt a lurch of excitement, but reined it in.

"I know," Noah said quietly, looking down to pick at imaginary lint on the blanket. "I just figured we needed some alone time to talk."

"Okay ..." Chynna paused several beats before saying, "Well, we're here, so ..."

Noah looked up at her again and this time, he looked her dead in the eye. "Listen, I'm sorry about what happened the other day in my bedroom. I was a real jerk. I shouldn't have behaved like that, and I'm sorry if I hurt you."

"You didn't hurt me, Noah."

Noah smiled and leaned over to tuck a tendril of hair that had escaped out of her cowboy hat behind her ear. "Are you sure about that? Because if I did, I would never forgive myself."

Chynna swallowed hard. "I'm sure."

An audible sigh of relief escaped those full lips of his. "I'm glad because I ..." He paused as if searching for the right words. "It was hard listening to what you had to say, but I think you had a point."

"You do?" Chynna was hopeful.

Noah nodded. "I've been stuck reliving the past for such a long time, I couldn't see the forest for the trees, but you've opened my eyes and made me see. You weren't afraid to stand up to me and call me out."

Chynna shrugged. "I hope I didn't offend you." It had been easy to stand up to Noah, but why was it so difficult in her everyday life?

"You didn't. And your outspokenness is one of the things I like about you, amongst other things. So basically, what I'm saying is, I like you Kenya. I like you a lot, and if you're willing, I would like another chance with you. You know, a fresh start."

Chynna knew what he meant, but she needed him to spell it out so there would be no misunderstandings. "A fresh start for what?"

Noah grinned and Chynna's heart skipped a beat. "For you and me, to figure out what's going on between us," he admitted honestly. "Because despite my boorish behavior that day, you and I both know that we've been circling each other for over a week. I'm hopelessly attracted to you, Kenya, and I guess what I'm saying very badly is that I'm tired of trying to fight it."

His compelling eyes riveted her to the spot but didn't prevent her from saying, "I'm attracted to you too, Noah Hart."

Noah reached for the picnic basket, fished out two flutes and passed them to her. "Hold these." He opened the bottle of sparkling cider he'd brought. He popped the cork on the cider and it nearly gushed over, but he caught it just in time to grab a flute and pour some in.

When they both had two full flutes, he toasted, "To a fresh start."

An undeniable magnetism was building between them, sending shivers of delight coursing through Chynna. "To a fresh start," she responded.

After they'd pigged out on hard salami, Brie, crackers, fruits and miniature dessert, they spread out on the blanket and Noah took Rylee's advice and asked Chynna to the anniversary party. "So will you come with me as my date to the Golden Oaks Ranch's thirty-fifth anniversary party this coming Saturday night?"

Chynna smiled at Noah. "I would love to."

"Good, I'll meet you in the foyer at six o'clock sharp."

"I'll be waiting."

ON SATURDAY NIGHT, as she got ready for her first official date with Noah, Chynna was a ball of nerves. Her stomach was in knots, and her palms were sweating. She'd never been this nervous about going out with a man before. Could it be because Noah was the first person she'd honestly cared about in years?

She'd taken care to dress for tonight. With Rylee's help, they'd ventured off the ranch for a few hours earlier that day to go back to the Canyon Ranch Spa. Chynna had informed the shocked hotel manager that she was checking out and would be taking all of her belongings. Although the woman seemed surprised by her attire of jeans, a plaid shirt and a cowboy hat, she was more pleased to see that after a week off the ranch, Chynna was unharmed and in good spirits.

Chynna had needed her luggage because inside were several of the clothes she and Kenya had bought during their shopping spree, and one of the dresses was perfect for the ranch's celebration that evening. It was a strapless, peach chiffon fit and flare dress that hit just above her knee. It was dressy without being too casual and simple enough not to be too flashy. She'd teamed it with dangling chandelier earrings and very minimal makeup, which was hard for Chynna. She was so used to being over the top that dressing down was somewhat of a challenge, especially with her hair. For concerts and club outings, it was the bigger the better. But for tonight, Chynna knew she wouldn't catch Noah's eye with her flare for the dramatic. Instead, she'd used some of Madelyn's old-fashioned hot rollers and the result was her hair hung in soft waves around her face.

Noah was used to seeing her hair in a ponytail or underneath a cowboy hat, so he was in for a surprise tonight. After a few spritzes of her favorite perfume, Chynna stared at herself in the mirror. *Here goes.*

She made her way down the circular staircase and found Noah waiting in the foyer. He looked up at her as she descended, and Chynna felt as a giddy as schoolgirl going to her first dance.

"You look amazing," Noah said when she made it to the last step.

"Thank you." Chynna beamed. "So do you." She knew most men preferred to be called handsome, but Noah truly was beautiful to her and not just because he was wearing a white tuxedo jacket and black pants. He wasn't just handsome—he had a good heart too.

He offered her his hand and together they walked into the living room where Madelyn, Isaac and Rylee were already gathered. Another young gentleman had joined the fold, and Chynna could only assume he was Rylee's date. He didn't at all appear to be Rylee's type.

"There you are," Madelyn said as they entered, but she stopped when she saw Chynna.

"Kenya, my darling, you look absolutely breathtaking."

"I would say so," Jeremy had muttered, and Chynna watched Rylee jab him in the middle with her elbow.

"Thank you, Mrs. Hart."

"And I see my son is accompanying you this evening?" Madelyn smiled at Noah and then back at Chynna.

Chynna didn't have to answer because Noah did. "Yes, Mother, and let's just let sleeping dogs lie."

Madelyn said knowingly, "Of course, come in you two. Would you like a glass of wine? Isaac, pour Kenya here a glass, will you, love?"

"Sure thing, babe." Isaac reached over on the cocktail table to pour Chynna a glass.

"Have you met Jeremy?" Madelyn asked, motioning to the man at Rylee's side.

"I don't believe I have," Chynna said, coming toward the couple.

"Jeremy's an old friend of the family," Noah said.

"And we're hoping it will turn into something more," Isaac said as he handed Chynna the wine goblet.

"Daddy, please," said Rylee, clearly exasperated by her family talking about her love life so freely. With her petite and slim figure, she looked darling in a one-shoulder jersey blouson mini-dress. Her spiral curls were pinned on each side of her face and hung down her back.

"Hey, what's wrong with wanting some grandchildren running around here?" Isaac inquired.

"I sure wouldn't mind having kids," Jeremy replied freely.

Chynna could see Rylee's obvious embarrassment and changed the subject. "So how many people are you expecting at the party tonight?" she asked, taking a sip of her Pinot Noir.

"Oh, hundreds," Madelyn said. "The mayor, city councilmen and members of the sheriff's department are coming."

"And what about our wayward son?" Isaac asked.

Chynna knew the Harts had a youngest son named Caleb, but he'd yet to show himself since her arrival on the ranch.

"Caleb will come," Madelyn replied somewhat testily.

"Mama, I wouldn't get your hopes up that Caleb will make an appearance," Noah said from Chynna's side. "I wouldn't want him to let you down."

"Does he always do that?" Chynna whispered in Noah's ear.

"He's the perpetual screw-up," Noah replied quickly.

"He knows how important this night is to me, to the family," Madelyn said, defending her youngest. "He'll show."

"If bull riding hasn't killed him yet," Isaac huffed underneath his breath.

"Why don't we start greeting our guests?" Rylee offered, to calm the situation between her parents. Whenever her youngest brother was mentioned, it always riled them up.

"That sounds like a good idea," Madelyn said as she swiftly placed her wineglass on the nearby cocktail table and headed for the door. "Are you coming?" She turned to her husband.

"Of course, my dear."

"I'm going to go keep the peace," Rylee said, heading toward the door. "I wouldn't want Caleb to ruin a perfectly good evening. Let's go, Jeremy." She grasped him by the arm and pulled him away, leaving Noah and Chynna alone.

"Your brother sounds like quite a hell-raiser, Noah," Chynna said.

"He is, and proud of it. But I don't want to think about him tonight." Noah pulled the wine goblet out of Chynna's hand and set it on the wet bar. "I want tonight to be about us."

Chynna looked into Noah's dark-brown eyes and knew that world had shifted. They were starting down a new path, and she couldn't wait to see what was around the other corner.

NOAH WATCHED Kenya as she mingled with the other guests chatting politics with several of the councilmen. They all seemed in awe of her; she had a special star quality that seemed to bedazzle men and women alike. Noah had been star-struck the moment they'd met, and tonight was no different. She was radiant *and* she was his for tonight.

"She's stunning," his father said from his side.

"I know," Noah replied huskily. He hadn't been able to think of anything else since he'd seen her walking down the steps tonight. She'd looked like an angel with her hair in soft curls and wearing very little makeup. The truth of the matter was Kenya didn't need it. She was naturally beautiful and the dress ... well, it was a dreamy confection of chiffon that showed off her elegance and grace. From someplace deep, he'd wanted to whisk her back up the stairs to his bedroom and finish what they'd started several days ago.

Isaac Hart stared at his son. "You're falling for her, aren't you?"

Noah blinked him back into focus. "What was that, Dad?"

His father laughed. "You're a goner."

"I don't know what you mean."

"You sure as hell do. From the day you brought that girl into this house, your mother and I have been waiting for you to realize what's been right in front of our faces."

"Which is?"

"That Kenya could be the woman to make you forget about Maya."

"I don't know if that will ever be possible, Dad."

"Sure it is," his father huffed. "You just have to be willing to allow it and let her in." Noah began to speak, but his father held up his hand. "Whoa there, let me talk for a minute." He grasped one of Noah's shoulders. "You and Kenya having a relationship does not change the fact that you loved and will always have a special place in your heart for Maya, but it's time you moved on, son. And that woman," he said, motioning with his beer bottle toward Chynna, who'd now gone out on the floor to dance with a seven-year-old boy, "is just the woman to do it."

CHYNNA GLANCED up to find Isaac and Noah staring at her as she danced with the young boy. The conversation looked intense, but she didn't have time to dwell on it, because Noah left his father standing at the edge of the dance floor and joined her.

"May I cut in, little man?" Noah asked, looking down at her escort.

"Huh?"

Noah bent down to the boy's height. "Well, I was hoping I could dance with the young lady here," he said, glancing up at Kenya.

"Is that alright with you, Miss Kenya?" the boy asked respectfully.

"Yes, that's fine, Andre."

"Okay, then," the boy said. "Save a dance for me later." He winked and rushed off the floor to join his family, seated at a table nearby.

Noah wasted no time in grasping Chynna's hand, pulling her into his arms and gliding her toward the center of the floor. "I guess I'm not the only man you've got wound up."

"Do I have you wound up?" Chynna inquired, her eyes wide with false innocence.

"Like a clock."

Noah laughed and Chynna's nerves instantly began to dissolve. Being in Noah's arms felt natural, as if she belonged there. It helped that Noah was a great dancer and spun her around and dipped her with ease. Eventually the music died down from the fast and furious line dancing to something soft and slow. That's when Noah slowed the pace, and they swayed gently to the music.

Chynna hazarded a glance at Noah, and he was staring down at her with such warmth she wanted to melt in a puddle at his feet, but he held her tight. One of his hands explored the hollows of her back while the other lightly stroked a wayward curl out of her face. He showered her with kisses, first on her forehead, then her jaw, before reaching her lips. When he did, he planted a tantalizing, slow and aching kiss across her lips.

She couldn't believe it. He was kissing her with his whole community watching; but she didn't care. She gave herself up to his persuasive mouth. The kiss was soft and sweet and held promise of a final mastery that was yet to come, but Chynna was certain she wanted to find out.

When he lifted his head, his eyes were dark and cloudy with passion. "You're so beautiful, Kenya," he said. "My sweet Kenya."

Hearing Noah say her sister's name made Chynna feel terrible for keeping the secret of her true identity from him. At the time, it had seemed like a smart idea, but she could have never imagined that the sexy rancher who'd rescued her would come to mean more to her than any man had in a long time.

So what now? Did she risk telling him the truth and enduring his wrath?

Noah kissed her again, and this time he slightly lifted her off her feet, making Chynna forget all about telling him the truth. She just wanted to bask in the moment of having this man adore her, for him to see her as more than just a pop icon or sex goddess. He saw in her the beautiful, strong, capable woman she knew she was.

With one of Noah's arms wrapped around her waist, they eventually left the dance floor. Chynna was eager for some time alone with Noah. *Perhaps in his room again.* But they were interrupted by a matronly woman and her husband. The clear look of disdain on the woman's face was evident, and Chynna tried not to recoil.

"Noah," the woman said.

Noah stiffened beside her, but finally spoke. "Mrs.

Jackson." He removed his hand from around her waist. He nodded his head to the man at her side. "Mr. Jackson."

Who is this woman and why is Noah pulling away from me? Chynna could feel the moment between them slipping away. *Why does this have to happen now?*

There was an awkward silence between all parties before Noah realized his social faux pas and said, "Allow me to introduce Kenya James."

Chynna offered her hand to the woman, but it was ignored, so she quickly snatched it back. Chynna tried to stay calm, but it was hard given the woman's obvious hostility toward her.

"H-How are you?" Noah attempted conversation.

"We're still grieving," the older man beside her answered as his wife shot Chynna poisonous looks.

"But clearly you've moved on," Mrs. Jackson spat.

"Hannah!" Chynna heard the warning in the man's voice beside her and that's when it hit her. These were Maya's parents, and Noah was making out with her in the middle of the dance floor where everyone could see. "I'm sorry if it upsets you. Truly I am, but I won't apologize for moving on with my life," Noah responded softly.

Chynna was happy to hear Noah defending their growing relationship. He wasn't ashamed of being with her.

"H-How could you?" Tears began to form in the older woman's eyes, and she blotted at them with a handkerchief she'd put in her purse. "It hasn't been that long."

"It's been over two years."

"Seems like it was just yesterday," Mr. Jackson said.

"I understand," Noah said. "But it's time. If you'll excuse us." He returned his hand to the small of

Chynna's back and led her away from the still-grieving couple.

Once they'd gone a safe distance, Noah pulled her away from the crowd. "I'm sorry about that," he said. "Those were my in-laws—Maya's parents.

"I figured as much."

"Mrs. Jackson had no right to treat you that way. It was incredibly rude."

"She's still grieving."

"That's no excuse. But I appreciate your understanding." Noah stroked her cheek. "You're really a special person, Kenya."

"And you're an amazing man." Chynna reached out and touched the strong line of his jaw.

"What do you say to some time alone?" Noah asked.

"I'd like that," Chynna said through mascara-coated eyelashes.

Noah grasped her by the hand and led her toward the main house.

12

"I need more heat!" the director of Chynna's newest video yelled at Kenya as she tried to act sexy in front of the camera in what wasn't more than a halter bikini top with some bootylicious shorts. Kenya was so embarrassed at the obvious sexploitation that she was having a hard time pulling off the video. She'd been unsuccessful in convincing Eli to change the vision.

She'd tried to contact Lucas, but he'd been out of the office. Now here she was in the middle of the night, filming this video. She was supposed to dance in the streets with her backup dancers and then frolic around in the pool with some model she'd met for all of five seconds. She was an actor and could do it; she just hated the image it presented of her sister.

"Cut!" the director said. "We'll take a break, and in that time, let's hope that our star here gets some chemistry with her leading man."

Eli, who'd been sitting in the background, stood back watching her while Deacon came forward.

"A word," Deacon said, grasping Kenya by the arm.

"What?" Kenya said, pulling away. She didn't need a pep talk from Deacon right now. More than anything, she had to act like Chynna and blow him off.

"I'm doing as he asked. What's his problem, anyway? He's not out there wearing next to nothing." She didn't wait for Deacon's response and instead stomped back toward her trailer.

Deacon was hot on her heels and rushed inside behind her. "What's your problem lately, Chynna? You've never been embarrassed before. You have a great body and truth be told, it's what everyone has come to expect from you."

"And does that make it right?"

Deacon stepped back and stared at Kenya. He seemed to be warring with himself for a quick comeback, and when he couldn't figure it out, he said, "Listen, let's just get through this video, and we'll talk to Eli about changing the concepts for the future videos."

Kenya was surprised that he'd conceded the point, but she was sure it was just in the name of getting the video shot. "Fine."

"Let's go."

"I'll be out in a minute," she said. She needed time to collect herself. She was going to have to use every ounce of the acting techniques she'd learned to get through this night; otherwise, Chynna's entire team would figure out that she wasn't the real deal if they hadn't already begun to suspect that.

"So you know what you need to do?" Eli asked Lamar Hobbs, Chynna's lover and former backup singer turned R&B bad-boy, from his limo sitting outside the mansion where they were taping.

As soon as Chynna had begun mouthing off on set, Eli had known he had to get her back on track. She was becoming much too mouthy and opinionated for his taste lately. Bringing back Lamar, the former love of her life, was sure to sex her up and have her off-kilter for a long time to come.

"Yeah," Lamar replied. "I got this." He knew exactly how to get through to Chynna. She'd always been putty in his hands. He knew how to hit all her buttons that would trigger the sexy Chynna James Eli needed.

KENYA SAT in her trailer in her robe, waiting for the call back to the set. She was eating a plate of grilled chicken breast and veggies that Fiona had brought, thanks to Deacon's close eye of watching her diet, when the trailer door swung open.

A fair-skinned man with Rico Suave hair and wearing jeans and a Rocawear T-shirt came bursting in.

"Hey, baby," he said with a wry smirk.

Kenya racked her brain for some memory of who this man could be. He seemed familiar, and he clearly knew her because he rushed over to sweep her in his arms and planted his hands on her behind.

His tongue plowed into her mouth as he kissed her with the finesse of a fourteen-year-old boy. Then his hands were everywhere. He pulled the robe down her shoulders as his mouth left her lips and he started nuzzling her neck. She didn't appreciate being manhandled, especially by someone with absolutely no skills, and she pushed at his chiseled chest. When he felt her resistance, he pulled away and looked at her strangely. His brow furrowed, and he frowned at her.

That's when it hit Kenya. He was Lamar Hobbs. The only man her sister had ever loved, but who'd also broken her heart by cheating on her and using her to further his own career. She'd made a tactical error by not at least faking the kiss and at least acting like she'd enjoyed it. She was going to have to seriously play this off. Otherwise, her and Chynna's entire plan was about to go up in smoke.

"Listen, Lamar," Kenya said. "You can't just come in here, kissing on me like the last three years didn't happen."

Lamar's mouth softened and he gave a half-smile. "I'm sorry, baby, but you know how it is in this business. I saw an opportunity and I took it."

"At my expense," Kenya replied huffily and turned away. She rolled her eyes upward and prayed for strength. She had to make this believable. When she finally turned around on cue, she'd found a way to wrestle up some fake tears and allow them to trickle down her cheeks. "What do you want, Lamar?"

"To make amends."

Lamar came toward her again, but Kenya had her arms folded squarely across her chest to prevent another attack of those wily hands.

"That's not possible."

"Oh c'mon, baby," Lamar responded in the sexy voice he used on the love ballads when he was crooning to a woman to take him back after he'd done wrong. "You and I were so good together, and we could be again."

When he reached for her this time, Kenya tried her best not to recoil from his touch. She tried to summon Lucas's face in her imagination, but she was having a hard time. "I don't think so," she said with a fake pout.

Lamar pulled her in his arms and stroked her cheek. "Think about how good we could be the second time around."

He leaned down to kiss her again, when a masculine voice said, "There won't be a next time." Lucas stood directly behind Lamar.

Stunned by the intrusion, but with his arm still circling Kenya's waist, Lamar turned around to face the intruder. "Well, if it isn't the great Lucas Kingston."

"Get your hands off her," Lucas said as he climbed the last step of the trailer.

Lamar must have heard the command in Lucas's tone, because he instantly released Kenya. He held up his hands in defense. "Sorry, man, I didn't realize you two," he said, pointing to Kenya, "Were the real deal. Thought it was all for the press."

"Well, it's real," Lucas stated. "So I would appreciate it if you didn't put your hands on my lady again. Capish?"

Lamar nodded. "It's cool, my man. I only showed up because Eli asked me to help loosen her up."

Kenya was floored by his comment. She couldn't believe that slimy weasel Eli had set her up. Lucas, on the other hand, was angered. He grabbed Lamar by his T-shirt. "What did you say?"

"Eli called me and asked me if I couldn't get your girl in check." He motioned to Kenya. "Said she's been a real pain to deal with these days."

"Don't you worry about Eli. I'll handle him." Lucas pointed his finger at Lamar. "You, on the other hand, should leave."

Lamar held up his hands in defense again. "Fine with me. Chynna and I had our moment, and it's been over for a minute."

"But you were willing to fake it?" Kenya finally found her voice. She was galled by his actions. *Is this really the kind of man Chynna had fallen for?* No wonder she needed to get away from her life for a while.

Lamar shrugged then turned on his heel and descended the trailer steps.

Kenya stared after him as if he were a unicorn that had suddenly materialized out of the blue. "I can't believe any of this." She shook her head in disbelief. "Eli sent Lamar here?"

"I'm sorry, Chynna. Eli was completely out of line, and I'm going to have a talk with him right now."

"What does he think?" Kenya's voice began to rise and her shoulders began to visibly shake. "That he can just pimp me out to the highest bidder?" Her mouth turned into an angry frown. "You can tell Eli I'm not for sale. Not now. Not ever."

"I'm truly sorry, and I promise I'll get him straightened out, but before I go, are you okay?" Lucas lifted her chin and forced to meet his gaze.

Usually with Lucas around, she was a ball of nerves, but right now all she could see was red. "I'm fine. I'd just like to be alone."

"Sure thing. Keep your head up. I know you'll finish strong."

LUCAS WAS RIGHT ABOUT one thing: Kenya knocked her performance out of the ballpark. She wouldn't give Eli the satisfaction of seeing her fail, so she'd walked into the next scene in the video full of fire and passion, so much so that she'd shocked the director.

"Cut!" he yelled.

They'd finally gone through each scene in one take without Kenya stopping and complaining. She just wanted the damn video to be over so she could go back to doing what she loved—and that was singing and most of all, acting. The best time of her experience playing Chynna was getting to act in her first motion picture—even if she was playing her sister.

Deacon quickly walked over with a robe to cover Kenya up. "Thanks." She gave him a half-hearted smile.

"You were full of fire before, so I don't know what happened during break," Deacon said, "but as always, you pulled through, perhaps because a certain mogul arrived?"

Deacon glanced in Lucas's direction, but he appeared to be having a heated discussion with his partner.

Kenya didn't answer. Instead, she stalked back to her trailer, desperate to remove the getup she'd been forced to wear. She had her twin to thank for this particular humiliation. Though deep down, Kenya wondered how Chynna would have truly behaved if Lamar had shown up out of the blue. *What would Chynna have done? Would she really have taken him back without a second glance?* Eli certainly seemed to think so, which showed Kenya just how little he respected her sister. Kenya had her work cut out for her making Chynna's record label and entourage see her as anything other than a sexy pop star.

"YOU HAD no right to bring Lamar here." Lucas was still arguing the point with Eli.

"Well, something had to be done. Chynna wasn't acting herself. You've seen it too. She's been different since she got back. The video was bombing because she was as stiff as ice, so I took action."

"The wrong action," Lucas replied. "You were wrong to bring that man here to play with her emotions."

"Maybe, but it worked, didn't it?" Eli pointed to the scene the crew was taking apart. "She changed her tune real quick."

"Not because of Lamar. *I* kicked him out."

Eli turned around to face him and looked him up and down. "So that was you, playa?" He gave a chuckle. "What exactly did you have to do to warm her up?"

Lucas was disgusted by Eli's connotation. "Chill with the innuendo. Nothing happened between me and Chynna."

"Yet."

"What do you mean, yet?"

"Lucas, c'mon. I'm your boy. I know when you have the hots for a babe and you want that broad real bad."

Lucas turned away, not because he was lying, but because he was telling the truth. He just refused to give Eli the satisfaction. It was his and Chynna's personal business if they chose to take their relationship to the next level. He certainly hoped so. Since she'd returned from Arizona, he'd had a raging hard-on. Not to mention the jealousy when he'd burst into Chynna's trailer to see Lamar manhandling her. He'd had to curb his desire to beat the crap out of that wanna-be Michael Jackson.

"You, "Lucas said, spinning around to face his oldest friend, "need to mind your own business."

"Hide it if you want," Eli said. "Won't change the facts that you got it bad." He started singing the Usher song "U Got It Bad" and moonwalking across the floor.

Lucas couldn't resist a chuckle. He could never stay mad at Eli for too long, even when he'd made some mistakes at the outset of starting the company. Eli had promised he would keep his eye on the ball, and he hadn't let him down since.

"Whatever, man," Lucas said. "Just don't pull any more stunts, ya hear?" He left Eli several minutes later in search of Chynna, but when he arrived at her trailer, he found it empty.

"Where's Chynna?" he asked Daisy, her makeup stylist who was packing up.

"Oh, she just left in the limo," Daisy said. "Appeared to be in a hurry."

Probably to get away from him, Lucas thought. But he'd had enough of their cat-and-mouse game. He was going to take a cue from Eli's playbook and take action.

The following day, he contacted Fiona and Deacon to finally arrange that date at Spago for him and Chynna, so they could be seen in public as a couple. It was a plausible excuse that would give Lucas time alone with Chynna without her entourage. But rather than tell Chynna about it, he'd informed Fiona that he wanted it to be a surprise. Better to catch Chynna off-guard than leave her with time to try and get out of their date. Fiona had been ecstatic as she'd been trying to arrange it since their return from New York. The only thing she didn't know is that he intended to take his and Chynna's relationship from public to personal—very personal.

When he showed up to Chynna's estate in his Ferrari, the security guard told him that it was Chynna's day off and that she was not seeing visitors, but Lucas was not taking "no" for an answer. He was determined to finish what they'd started that night in the limo after his birthday party. He used strong-arm tactics to convince the guard to let him in against Chynna's wishes, which is why Chynna swung open the door in a sexy cami and boy shorts and looked disgruntled.

"I told you I didn't want ..." Her voice trailed off

when she saw Lucas standing on the other side of the door. "What are *you* doing here?"

"I came to take you out on that date," Lucas said, eyeing her in the shorts that showed off her ample, but toned, thighs—thighs he wanted wrapped around him tonight.

"Date?" She looked perplexed.

He was sure she was racking her brain, trying to see if she'd forgotten an appointment.

"Our public date that Fiona planned for Spago," he offered.

"But we hadn't set a date yet."

"We have now." He stepped past her and into the foyer.

"I didn't invite you in."

"I invited myself."

Chynna folded her arms across her chest. "I'm sorry, but I'm not interested in going out tonight. I've rather had enough of putting myself on show recently."

"Put on whatever you want," Lucas said. "Whatever you'll be comfortable in, but we're going out. Me and you. No entourage."

She tried to interrupt him with "buts," but he ignored her. "Go put something on." He pushed her toward the grand staircase. "I'll be here waiting for you."

Kenya stood firmly in the middle of the foyer, pouting.

"I'm not leaving here without you," Lucas said, "so you might as well go get dressed."

She sighed heavily, but eventually spun on her heel and began running up the stairs. She knew she couldn't be caught dead not looking her best, so she slipped into an animal print sheath dress and grabbed her Missoni coat and Jimmy Choo clutch. She piled her hair in a simple, sleek ponytail.

"This is as good as it's going to get," Kenya said when she descended the staircase, fifteen minutes later.

After he'd assessed her for several long moments, he said, "You look beautiful in anything you wear." And he meant every word. She looked young and sweet and sexy at the same time.

"C'mon." He grabbed her by the hand and led her out to his Ferrari. He was excited about the wonderful evening he had planned as he opened the door and she slid inside. She was his prisoner for the night, and she had no idea that tonight would be the night they became lovers.

THE PAPARAZZI WERE hot on their heels for the first few miles, but Lucas knew he could lose them in his Ferrari. So when they drove up to valet parking outside Spago, they were paparazzi-free.

After the valet had taken Lucas's keys with a terse warning from him to be careful, Lucas led her inside. The maître d' sat them in a private booth to enjoy their meal in peace. Soon, the waiter was returning with a bottle of Cristal, which Lucas nodded for him to open.

Lucas picked up his glass first. "To a great evening."

Kenya managed a tremulous smile, even though her heart was thudding and hadn't settled into a natural rhythm since he'd showed up unannounced at her door. "To a great evening." She clicked her flute against his.

"You know, you can relax," Lucas said, sitting back

against the booth's cushions and assessing her frankly. "I'm not going to bite unless you want me to."

"I'll be sure and let you know when I'm ready for you to," she surprised herself by saying.

Lucas grinned broadly and took a sip of his champagne. "I think tonight is going to be a great night."

And to Kenya's surprise, it was. Once the champagne had begun to work its magic and ease her nerves at being alone with a man she was immensely attracted to, the conversation flowed easily. And the food ... well, Kenya enjoyed every bit of her sweet corn soup, fresh vegetable salad and wild king salmon while Lucas had indulged in soft shell crab and a dry-aged New York steak from the famous restaurant.

They talked about music and shared a love of a variety of it, from jazz to country to rhythm and blues. Eventually they talked about the movie Chynna was filming and how much she didn't care for acting.

"But it's a natural step for you in today's market," Lucas said.

"I know that. But it doesn't come easy for me."

"You convinced Carter Wright to keep you."

"That's because my back was against the wall, and I always come out fighting."

"You impressed me."

Kenya laughed. "And after all these years I thought that was an impossible task."

Eventually, their conversation flowed to a more personal nature, and Lucas shared with her his roots and upbringing.

"It wasn't easy getting out of South Central," he said. "The odds were in my favor of becoming another statistic of a young black man in jail, but I had a different future in mind. Going to college and getting a degree were part of it."

"What made you decide to get into the record business versus going corporate after you got your MBA? The music business can be so fickle."

"In one word ... Eli," Lucas said. "The man had been singing and dancing since we were kids. When were in high school, Eli could always spot when someone had talent. He formed his own band, and I even thought they might get picked for a record label themselves, but that day never materialized. When I graduated UCLA, Eli pitched starting a record label together. It was a long shot, I knew. But then again, my getting out of South Central alive with no babies with a degree in my hand had been too."

"So you took a chance?" Kenya asked.

Lucas nodded. "And it paid off big-time. Signing you was one of the best moves Eli ever made."

Kenya nodded. "You're right about that. You snapped me up before any of the big boys could get to me."

"And I'm glad we did." Lucas studied her face unhurriedly.

"What?" she asked. She could see he was deep in thought, but about what she didn't know.

"I've underestimated you," he said, finally. "Always thought you were all flash and sass, but you've surprised me in so many ways." His eyes raked over her boldly as he leaned closer on the table toward her. "There are so many different sides to you that I feel like I've barely touched the surface."

It had been a long time since a man had looked at her the way Lucas was doing at that moment. He was making her feel special and desirable, which is why, in an uncharacteristic move, she scooted toward him in the booth, wrapped one arm around his neck and pulled him closer.

She stared deep into his eyes for a long moment, trying to assess if she could trust him ... if she could trust herself. Finding her answer, she boldly pressed her lips against his. She stroked them softly until he pulled her more firmly to him.

Their mouths melded together, each giving and taking what the other offered—lips, tongues and more. It was a sweet, sensuous kiss that seemed to last forever. When they finally pulled apart, they were breathless.

"What do you say we get out of here?" Lucas whispered huskily.

Kenya nodded. Her mind told her to wait and be cautious, but her body was aflame and it was time she finally put out the spark.

After he took care of the bill, Lucas slowly rose to his feet and held out his hand to help her up. Brushing her dress when she stood, Kenya suddenly felt self-conscious that she'd just agreed to go to bed with Lucas. Apparently, he had no qualms. Touching the back of her spine, he propelled her forward and outside the hotel where his Ferrari awaited them.

The ride to Lucas's penthouse was quiet yet fraught with sexual tension. Kenya didn't know who was more nervous—her or Lucas. Or maybe it was just excitement. It certainly was for her. It had been several years since she'd been with a man. Her last relationship had ended with a sputter because Jason hadn't been the "one" for her. Although they'd enjoyed each other's company and liked the same activities, there just wasn't a spark between them. When Kenya had eventually ended the relationship, there hadn't been any crying or theatrics. They'd parted as friends, wishing each other the best of luck.

That wasn't the kind of relationship Kenya wanted.

She wanted fire and passion. Sparks. She certainly had those with Lucas. She wasn't sure if there was more beyond the physical attraction, though tonight he had shown her there was a lighter, more fun side to him than she'd imagined.

When the car came to a stop in front of his modern two-story duplex, Kenya's nerves suddenly attacked. Her stomach clenched, and she could feel her pulse racing.

As if sensing her uneasiness, Lucas turned to her but didn't shut off the engine. Kenya looked down at the car floor. "Look at me, Chynna."

Slowly, her eyes rose to meet his dark gaze. "I want to sleep with you, Chynna. There's no denying that, but this has to be consensual. If you come upstairs with me, you need to be sure this is want you want. Otherwise, if you're having second thoughts, I can turn the car around and take you home."

His words were so sincere and his gaze so honest that any fear or doubts Kenya had slipped away. Somehow she found her voice and said, "I want you too."

Lucas smiled that devilishly handsome smile that made her heart go pitter-pat, and he turned off the engine.

Several minutes later, they'd walked the stairs to his condo and just as he opened the door, he pulled her into his arms and spun her inside. He backed her against the door as he shut it and kissed her until she was dizzy with passion. She didn't have time to recover from his assault before he was pulling at the Missoni coat she wore and tossing it to the floor.

Kenya lifted her legs around his waist, and Lucas caught her in his arms and carried her through the condo. She assumed they were heading into his bedroom, but instead he lowered her onto the rug in the center of the room.

Before joining her on the rug, he looked down at her. "You have no idea how beautiful you are, do you?"

Even though she knew he thought he was talking to Chynna, she loved being complimented. Although Chynna had always been in the limelight and called one of the most beautiful women in the world in magazines, Kenya had never thought of herself as beautiful. It was funny given that they shared the same face. Maybe people were right about the self-confidence thing—how it could make you appear more beautiful.

She reached for both sides of Lucas's face and pulled him down onto the bearskin rug with her. Their bodies sank into the plush rug, her soft curves against his hard, strong masculine body. They kissed, touched and caressed each other, but hadn't removed a stitch of clothing. It was utterly erotic and completely baffling. She'd thought, given his franticness a moment ago, that it was going to be a fiery session, but instead he'd calmed himself and was taking his time to get to know every curve of her body.

And when he'd had his fill, he finally tugged at the zipper of the animal print dress she wore and tugged it down to her waist, leaving her upper body bare to his gaze. This wasn't the first time he'd seen her this way. The only difference was that this time, she wouldn't run away. This time she would go for it.

He lowered his head so he could kiss her alert nipples. A light ripple flowed through her at his featherlight kisses. And when his tongue came to one chocolate areola and licked and flicked at it with the tip of his tongue before taking the peak in his mouth, she began to pant and her chest heaved.

He laved one breast with his mouth and tongue

while his other hand moved magically over the other. He thumbed a nipple deliciously, up and down with his fingers, bringing it to a hardened pebble, so he could lean over and give it the same attention he'd given the first. Kenya squirmed underneath him, but that didn't stop his pursuit. He slipped his hands downward to her dress, bunched at her hips, and hooked his fingers inside her thong and slid them down her hips.

Slowly, but surely, he edged his finger inside her and she bucked against his featherlight touch.

"Chynna," he groaned when his fingers came back dewy with her moisture.

"Yes," Kenya moaned, wanting more of the delicious friction his fingers promised, and he didn't disappoint. They tormented her with exquisite tenderness until she became wet and nearly crested.

That's when he lifted up for the merest of seconds to pull his T-shirt over his head and tossed it aside while she slid out of the remainder of her dress. He was magnificently cut and toned. She'd never seen him without his shirt before, although she'd felt his muscular proportions underneath the clothes he wore. She couldn't resist tapping her fingers down his chest in rainfall patterns seconds before he lay atop her and crushed her breasts against the hardness of his chest, but it felt oh-so- good, not to mention the drugging kiss he gave her, which sent new spirals of ecstasy coursing through her.

She reached for the buckle on his jeans and began working the belt free. When she felt it give way, she lowered the zipper, and this time, she returned the favor by reaching inside the waistband of his briefs to cup him in her hands. She heard his sharp intake of breath as she stroked his hard length.

"Chynna, oh Chynna," he murmured into her hair as she stroked him and deepened the kiss by thrusting her tongue into his mouth. She'd never been this take-charge in the bedroom, but there was something about Lucas that told her she was free to do whatever, wherever with him.

Kenya continued to stroke his hard length until he grasped her hand and slowly pulled her away. "Easy, love, if you continue down this path, I won't be much good to you later."

"Don't tell me you're a five-minute man," Kenya teased.

"Oh, no, I just prefer to be inside when I come," Lucas responded.

Kenya was shocked by his boldness, but not enough to stop what was about to happen. She'd never been this attracted to a man so quickly before, but something told her that pure pleasure awaited her.

"Well, then let's see about getting you naked," she responded and caressed his jeans down his legs. Lucas did the rest by toeing off his shoes and socks until he too was as naked as she, but instead of joining her, he left her side momentarily. He returned with several packets of condoms.

Thank goodness he was thinking logically enough to protect the two of them. She'd been so caught up in the moment that she hadn't thought of the consequences of having unprotected sex. She needn't have worried, because Lucas was protected and poised above her within seconds.

All thoughts scattered of anything else other than this man and this moment. He spread her legs wide, and Kenya felt the thick pressure of him at her center then his thrusts full and deep inside her. Her breath hitched as her body got accustomed to his length. He thrust again, harder and deeper until she *felt* him and sensations began to whirl in her body. He filled her so perfectly, so completely.

When Lucas looked down into her eyes, she locked his gaze and began to move underneath him. She rolled her hips in an erotic dance that Lucas followed just as he had done that night when they'd danced at his birthday party. Except this time, they were taking it to the ultimate level that two people could share.

She wrapped her legs around his waist and he took the cue, thrusting harder, faster, accelerating the pace. Kenya looped her arms around his neck and brought his mouth down on hers. The warm sweep of his tongue inside hers as his lower body thrust into her engaged all of Kenya's senses. She flamed hotter and hotter. So hot, she thought she might burn out, but Lucas didn't let her. Right when she was on the brink of coming, he slowed the pace. Her head lolled, and she arched her back off the floor.

Lucas used it as an opportunity to switch positions. Now she was on top, her hair trailing across his broad chest, and her legs straddling his hips as she pulled him deep inside her body. He gathered her hair in his hands, massaging, seducing and combing with his fingers. It was highly seductive, and she gazed down at him. His eyes were glazed with passion. She began to move over him, and she could see the tendons straining in his neck as he tried to keep control. She braced her hands against his chest while her thighs gripped his hips and she rode him higher and higher.

"Chynna ... Jesus, what are you doing to me?"

Lucas moaned. He caressed one of her breasts and plucked and teased them between his fingers.

"I'm going to make you come," Kenya said boldly, mimicking his earlier words.

"You first," Lucas said. Just then, he slid his fingers to find the place where earlier he'd turned her into an aching bundle of nerves and left her hanging, except this time, he skillfully circled his thumb around the hub of her femininity and she shuddered. "Lucas!" she screamed as the room spun around her and the boundary between the two of them fell way.

He gripped her hips and gave one final thrust. Seconds later, Kenya felt his fierce shudders reverberating throughout her entire body as he went over the edge. His completion sent another round of flashing lights in her head, and she came cascading back down to earth.

ON THE OTHER side of town, Eli met up with Lamar at a dive bar on Sunset Boulevard. The bar was known for its less than favorable clientele, but that was just fine with Eli. He didn't want to be seen in a more well-known establishment because it might get back to Lucas that he hadn't stopped interfering in Chynna's business.

"Hey, man, thanks for meeting me," Eli said when Lamar slid into a booth beside him.

Lamar was wearing all black, a baseball hat and sunglasses, even though they were inside. "What's up with all the cloak and dagger shit?" Lamar asked. "My agent would kill me if she knew I was in this place."

Eli shrugged. "Hey, I helped you get signed with her, didn't I?"

"Yeah, and in case you hadn't forgotten," Lamar said, "it cost me."

Eli hadn't forgotten. Three years ago, he'd seen Chynna and Lamar getting way too close for comfort. He wanted to keep Chynna focused on the prize of becoming the next pop diva. He'd had to do something. Once he recognized Lamar would give up love for money and fame, the rest had been easy. On the down low, he'd helped Lamar find a record deal and an agent. Soon, Lamar was saying bye-bye to Chynna in favor of finding his own fame. Chynna had been devastated by Lamar's betrayal, especially because her mama had just died. Even though he'd tried putting several men in front of her—directors, actors other musicians—Eli doubted she'd ever truly gotten over Lamar. So yes, the boy owed him big-time.

"Well, what I want to know is what happened between you and Chynna," Eli said. He had just known if he threw Lamar back into the mix, Chynna would become a bowl of mush.

"That's the thing, dude. I don't know what happened."

"What do you mean?"

"I mean she wasn't herself," Lamar replied. "If you ask me, she acted like she didn't even recognize me."

Eli's forehead furrowed into a frown. "What do you mean *she didn't recognize you*?"

"I don't know. I can't put my finger on it. For a few minutes, when I was trying to rap to her, she was completely blank. No emotion whatsoever. She was like a stranger. And then just as quickly, it was over, and she was pushing me away and giving me shit for kicking her to the curb."

Eli rubbed his chin thoughtfully. "You don't say." This was an interesting wrinkle. *Why would Chynna act like she didn't know her one and only love? The one man she'd said she couldn't live without?* It didn't make sense. *What's going on*? Eli had to find out. Someway, somehow, he would get to the bottom of it because the only thing he was willing to accept was the old Chynna, who did what he what wanted, how he wanted and anywhere he wanted it.

13

Just as Noah and Kenya were walking toward the main house for some private time, he heard a loud scream. It sounded like it was coming from Rylee. He stiffened almost immediately and began scanning the crowd for some sign of his sister in distress. When he found Rylee, she wasn't in danger. She was kissing their wayward brother, who'd finally arrived nearly two hours late to the ranch's celebration.

"What's going on?" Kenya asked from his side with concern.

"Oh, that's just Caleb, my younger brother," said Noah. "Apparently, he's finally decided to grace us with his presence after three months. I'll introduce you."

Noah sensed Kenya's alarm and said quietly, "Don't worry. Caleb will love you. He loves all the ladies."

He squeezed her hand and walked her over toward where his parents, Rylee, Jeremy and Caleb were standing in a semicircle.

"Oh, thank God you're home," Madelyn Hart said to Caleb as Noah approached. "I've missed you so."

"Well, I'm here, Mama," Caleb said, rushing into

her welcome arms. "Just like I told you I would be." He glanced over at Noah, expecting a reaction, but Noah wasn't going to give him any. He'd had plenty of drama tonight from his former in-laws.

Noah could, however, see the dismayed look flash across his father's face at Caleb's appearance. He wondered what Kenya thought of his rebellious younger brother.

CHYNNA WAS a bundle of nerves at Noah's side. *Could lightning strike twice and Caleb not recognize her either, like Noah?* She glanced at Noah's younger brother. Caleb was the exact opposite of Noah, thought Chynna. Noah was classically good-looking, but Caleb was a sexy rake with low-cut hair and a wide grin. He was wearing dirty rodeo chaps over snug-fitting jeans, sported a smudged white shirt, snakeskin boots and a cowboy hat atop his head.

"Caleb." Madelyn was eying him warily. "You didn't have time to change?" She glanced around the party, and they had several onlookers. "We do have guests."

Caleb shrugged. "You wanted me on time, didn't you?" He glanced at Noah. He raised an eyebrow at the woman on his side. Noah had a date? *Who is she?* She looked oddly familiar.

"Go change, boy," Isaac said, interrupting Caleb's thoughts.

"Will do, sir." Caleb gave a quick nod to everyone before departing to the main house. He determined that when he came back, he would have another look at the arresting woman at Noah's side.

"I think we should have a drink," Madelyn said to

Chynna, "while we wait for Caleb to join us. Then we'll have a proper toast."

Chynna sighed inwardly. Clearly, she and Noah were not going to get that alone time they were after—at least not tonight.

"What do you say?" Noah asked, turning to her. Was it her imagination, or was he as disappointed as she that they wouldn't get their time together?

"I would love a vodka tonic." She really wanted a glass of red wine, but vodka had very little calories, and she had to keep herself fit and trim for when she returned to her tour.

"I'll go get it." Noah left her to go to the far side of the party where a bartender was set up.

When he exited, it dawned on Chynna that she hadn't thought of her career in days. She'd been so fixed on the ranch and Noah, heck the entire Hart family that she'd forgotten that a life awaited her in Los Angeles. She hadn't spoken to Kenya in days, and she had no idea what was going on. She assumed everything was okay. Otherwise, Kenya would be calling her in a panic. *Has Kenya finally become accustomed to living my life? What does her silence mean?* Most of all, she was falling for Noah Hart. In a short time, he'd crept inside her heart and made her want to know what it would be like to be loved by this man. Eventually, something would have to give, but what?

"You're deep in thought," Rylee said when she came up to Chynna while her pseudo-suitor was speaking with her parents. "What's wrong?"

Chynna shrugged. "I was just thinking how much fun I'm having here."

Rylee understood what Chynna *wasn't* saying and finished her sentence, "But that it will have to come to an end soon?"

Chynna nodded. Warning signs of alarm were erupting inside of her.

"Who says it has to?" Rylee replied. "Tell Noah who you are. I'm sure the two of you can figure something out."

"Rylee, my life is in L.A., and I'm always on the go. Noah's life is here on the ranch. He wouldn't fit in my world. It would be like trying to fit a round peg into a square hole."

"True, but you won't know until you try."

"I suppose you're right," Chynna said in a small, frightened voice, "but I'm afraid of how he'll react when he realizes I've been deceiving him about who I am."

Rylee grabbed Chynna by the arm. "*You* are still *you*. The Chynna he's gotten to know is just another side of you that the public doesn't see."

"When you put it like that, it makes it sound easy. I'm not sure of how Noah will take the news."

"Take what news?" Noah said from behind Rylee, and Chynna flinched at the sound of his voice. He handed Chynna her drink, and their eyes connected when their hands touched for a fraction of a second as she accepted the glass.

Luckily, Rylee covered and said, "That Caleb said he's going to stay awhile."

Noah chuckled. "What, a week? You know that boy can't stay in one place for any length of time. He's got wanderlust in his eyes, and I don't see that changing anytime soon or at least not until he meets the right woman."

He looked at Chynna with such longing that Rylee cleared her throat. "Excuse me. I'm just going to get Jeremy and prevent him from talking Mama and Daddy's ear off."

Seconds later, she was gone and it was just Chynna and Noah again. "I'm sorry we keep getting interrupted," Noah said. "Perhaps it's the universe's way of telling us to slow things down." If they hadn't been stopped by his in-laws and Caleb's arrival, Noah knew where they would be right now—naked and between the sheets.

"There's always later." Chynna smiled mischievously.

Noah was about to comment when Caleb returned in a clean shirt, jeans and wearing the same snakeskin cowboy boots as before. "The prodigal son is back," Noah said, walking toward his brother, but then Caleb stopped dead in his tracks as he came face-to-face with Chynna and truly saw her for the first time. "Why didn't anyone tell me we had a celebrity in our midst? If you had, I would have dressed better."

"What are you talking about, Caleb?" Madelyn asked.

"C'mon." Caleb laughed incredulously, looking back and forth between his parents and siblings. "Don't tell me none of you knew you were having cocktails with *the* Chynna James." He turned to Rylee. "C'mon, sis, you have all her music."

Noah turned to Chynna, and her entire face blanched. That's when he stared directly at Rylee, but his sister hung her head low too ... and that's when Noah knew Caleb was telling the truth. The woman who'd been a part of his family for weeks, would he'd been falling for, been about to make love to, had been lying to him about her real identity as a pop star?

Noah fixed his eyes on the woman of the hour, willing her to tell him the truth. "It's true, isn't it?"

"I'm so, so sorry for the deception," the words tumbled out of Chynna's mouth.

"*Really*?" Noah snapped.

"Yes, really." She turned to face Madelyn and Isaac. "I've wanted to tell you the truth." Tears welled in her eyes. "But you see, my life has been in turmoil, carried out in the media for the entire world to see. I,I just needed a little reprieve from the real world for a world for a while, so I used my twin's name, Kenya, instead of telling you my real name, which is Chynna James."

"I'll say," Caleb replied. "You probably wanted to get away from all those folks calling you a slut and a homewrecker."

"Caleb!" His mother was horrified by his bad manners.

"I'm just repeating what the press said weeks ago. They had pictures of her," he said, nodding toward Chynna, "kissing a married man."

"I am not a homewrecker!" Chynna stomped her feet. She couldn't believe the progress that she'd made with Noah was about to slip through her fingers. "None of what they wrote is true." She faced Noah with pleading eyes. "Just because the press writes a fiction doesn't make it fact."

"Then how did they get photos?" Noah asked. Although he hadn't seen them, it sounded awfully suspicious. And where there was smoke ... Chynna stared at Noah several long moments. She could see in his eyes that his image of her was tarnished. *Will he ever look at me the same?* She gave a horrified cry and ran toward the main house.

Noah turned a murderous look on Caleb.

"Listen, I'm sorry, okay?" Caleb's voice softened at seeing a beautiful woman in distress. "I was just running my mouth off at what the tabloids say. How was I to know she hadn't told you the truth? I mean, you are dating her, are you not?"

Noah stared at Caleb with bewilderment. For the first time, Caleb was right about one thing. He'd been falling for a woman he didn't really know. A woman who'd lied and deceived him about who she truly was. And if she was lying to him about something as simple as her real name, what other secrets was Chynna hiding?

He stared at her retreating figure and wondered, *Can I believe anything that happened between us in the last two weeks?* Or was it all just a lie or a figment of his imagination? *Who is the real Chynna?*

BOOKS BY YAHRAH ST. JOHN

Connected Books

One Magic Moment

Dare to Love

Dirty Laundry Series

Dirty Laundry

Can't Get Enough

Stand Alone Novels

Never Say Never

Risky Business of Love

Hart Series

Entangled Hearts

Entangled Hearts 2

Untamed Hearts

Restless Hearts

Unchained Hearts

Chasing Hearts Pub Date

Captivated Hearts

Mitchell Brother Series

Claimed by the Hero

Seducing the Seal

Coming Soon in 2022

Guarding His Princess

ABOUT THE AUTHOR

Yahrah St. John became a writer at the age of twelve when she wrote her first novella after secretly reading a Harlequin romance. Throughout her teens, she penned a total of twenty novellas. Her love of the craft continued into adulthood. She's the proud author of thirty-nine books with Harlequin Desire, Kimani Romance and Arabesque as well as her own indie works.

When she's not at home crafting one of her spicy romances with compelling heroes and feisty heroines with a dash of family drama, she is gourmet cooking or traveling the globe seeking out her next adventure. For more info: www.yahrahstjohn.com or find her on Facebook, Instagram, Twitter, Bookbub or Goodreads.

Printed in the USA
CPSIA information can be obtained
at www.ICGtesting.com
LVHW030034220823
755846LV00009B/701